T0207634

# Lakeview Park

Other titles by the author, written with Lorna Collins:

*31 Months in Japan: the Building of a Theme Park*
*Murder... They Wrote*
*Murder in Paradise*

Editor: Lorna Collins

# Lakeview Park

## A Short Story Collection

## BY LARRY K. COLLINS

iUniverse, Inc.
Bloomington

# LAKEVIEW PARK
## A Short Story Collection

*iUniverse books may be ordered through booksellers or by contacting:*

*iUniverse*
*1663 Liberty Drive*
*Bloomington, IN 47403*
*www.iuniverse.com*
*1-800-Authors (1-800-288-4677)*

*ISBN: 978-1-4620-7000-8 (sc)*
*ISBN: 978-1-4620-7001-5 (ebk)*

*Printed in the United States of America*

*iUniverse rev. date: 12/02/2011*

# Dedication

~for Lorna, my wife, lover, and best friend
who believes in me and also corrects my spelling
and punctuation ~

# Contents

# Clarence

Clarence pulled his grimy blue sweatshirt closer about him, hoisted the black plastic bag to his shoulder and started across the grass toward the next trashcan, following the walking path along the lakefront. His mood matched the day, gray and overcast. A cold February wind ruffled the waters. Even the ducks were huddled in the protection of the trees far from the water. Only a lone egret waded at the south end, scanning the shallows for fish.

"Just you and me, Tall Skinny Kid," Clarence mused, for that's what he'd come to call the white bird with the long neck. *You and me going about our noontime rituals: you walking the shallows with your tail dragging in the pond; me collecting cans and bottles to turn in for food money. How long has it been? Seems like an eternity.*

Clarence paused, set the bag down and watched the lone unmoving figure stare into the wind-rippled water. *Has it really been that long?* He thought back, trying to focus. *I got canned last May and now it's almost March; that's ten months.* He shook his head. *Hardly seems possible.*

"Doesn't look like a good day for either of us, Skinny Kid. Too much wind for you to spy dinner and too cold for most regular folks to be here."

"Well, tomorrow's Wednesday. Should be better. The RC sailboat club meets down on the peninsula. Any time there's wind, they show up. Those old guys sit in their folding chairs along the edge, fingering joysticks while their sailboats jockey for position around the flags. They always leave empties, though. Yep, tomorrow should be better."

He again hoisted the half-empty sack and trudged toward the next container. Reached in to retrieve two Diet Pepsi cans.

"Slim pickins," he said to no one, since no one was around. Clarence had developed this habit of talking to himself. Better than the constant silence.

"Can't hardly wait for spring. Warm weather and people picnicking. Ah... and those company parties around the fire pits. Them folks always provide. Sometimes they even leave leftover hot dogs and potato salad. Then I can use my recycle money for gas for Big White Truck. Yeah, can't hardly wait."

Clarence's monologue was interrupted by a commotion from the far side of the upper lake. The geese were making a racket.

"Either the 'feathered mafia' have spotted Jorge or there's a dog loose in the park." Clarence called the five large geese that ruled the upper lake near the island bridge, the 'feathered mafia.' Then Clarence saw Jorge.

Jorge Garcia came around noon every day. Rain, cold, heat, didn't matter. He always wore short pants, a dirty red sweatshirt and carried three shopping bags: one filled with heads of lettuce, one with day-old bread, and the third with birdseed.

You'd have thought the Pied Piper of Hamlin had arrived the way the entire flock would surround him, hundreds of ducks, geese, some visiting mallards, and a multitude of black-feathered, white-beaked mud hens. Through this fowl mass, the 'feathered mafia' would stroll unchallenged to be first served. The rest would then fight over the remainder. Seagulls circled above. They didn't seem to be hungry, but let a mud hen try to escape with a large piece of bread and they would descend to separate the poor bird from his dinner. Successful, they often tossed the stolen morsel away. The chase being better than the prize.

By the time Clarence reached the upper lake, the show was about over. Jorge had cast the last of the seed into the air and was headed back to the parking lot. The flock dispersed in all directions.

Crossing the bridge, Clarence encountered several power walkers doing laps on the one-kilometer-long asphalt path that circled the lake. They paid no attention to him, and he didn't make eye contact. A girl, she looked about high school age, jogged by in a gray-hooded tee, matching tights, and short, white skirt. White ear buds connected to the iPod at her waist. Clarence's eyes followed her up the path for a short distance, and then he turned slowly back to the task at hand.

How long had it been? The divorce was five years ago. Before that he had been happily married, well more like comfortably married, with a reasonably steady job and a future. The drink had messed that up. First Margaret, then finally the job disappeared. Now he lived in his truck and collected recycle for the deposit money. But he was sober, hadn't had a drink in six months.

"Hey, Yosemite Sam, what you doing?"

Clarence looked up from the waste receptacle to see four kids from the local mid-high school.

"Punks." He whispered to himself. This group often harassed him. Last fall the local youth gang had nicknamed him 'Yosemite Sam,' probably because of the matted shoulder-length hair and gray beard reaching to his chest.

"Why ain't you in school?" he called back.

"Don't you know, old man, it's Presidents' Day. No school," said the ringleader, a heavyset kid with baggy pants hung so low that the elastic band of his shorts was perpetually exposed above his belt.

*Fortunately there are only four of them today. Not enough to harass me,* Clarence thought. *It took ten punks last summer.* The group had surrounded him, grabbed his recycle bag and after tiring of 'keep away,' tossed it into the lake. Wouldn't happen today, though; these kids were only brave in larger numbers.

"Was a time when I could have taken all you punks," he murmured to himself. In high school he'd been on the football team, his five-foot ten-inch frame all buff and muscular. But life on the street had taken its toll on him. Now thinner, he'd had to punch three more holes in his belt over this past year.

Clarence ignored the catcalls and insults and continued his rounds. As he reached the south end, he again encountered the egret. It hadn't moved.

"Have patience, dear friend," he whispered toward the still bird. "It's getting close to month end. The Fish and Game people should do their monthly restocking any day now."

It was always lively for several days following a restocking. Fishermen would line the banks. Still, there'd be plenty of fish for the egret and plenty of recycle from the fishermen. Then, somehow word would get to the cormorants, which would magically appear in groups of fifty or more. They would sweep the lake in military precision, heads popping up to look skyward then disappearing beneath the surface again. Within several days of their appearance, the fish, fishermen, and cormorants would all be gone, leaving the lonely shore to Tall Skinny Kid, and himself.

As Clarence watched, the egret's head slowly moved back, coiling the long neck. Then, STRIKE. With blurring speed the head descended and up came the beak, holding a small fish. A quick toss and the morsel disappeared into the mouth and down the throat.

"Good work, Tall Skinny Kid," Clarence called. The egret seemed to take a small bow before resuming his frozen posture above the shallow water. "Your luck's changing; maybe mine will, too."

Brightened by his friend's good fortune, Clarence headed for the last trash container, the one just before the parking lot and public restrooms. It was usually one of the better locations. Today was no exception. He found several large glass bottles, the high value ones, in addition to two six-packs of empty cans.

"Someone had a nice party, and me an' Big White Truck thank you," Clarence said to the empty air. This haul, along with the earlier run would insure a meal and maybe a little left over for gas.

"Maybe my luck's changing too."

Big White Truck waited in the lot near the men's room. It was the last major item Clarence could call his own. He had bought the 1989 Ford Ranger 4x4 years ago at a time when he was flush with money. The previous owner had modified it by raising the body higher to accommodate oversize tires. This made it somewhat top heavy, but Clarence loved it. From high up in the cab he could look down on other drivers. A metal step bar had been added below each door to make it easier to climb in. Even so, Margaret had refused to ever ride in it.

"It's too tall and too ugly," she'd complained. She continuously nagged him to get rid of the monstrosity. It was about the only thing his wife hadn't gotten from the divorce.

Now it was both transportation and his home. Big White Truck couldn't stay at the park overnight; the local police patrolled after dark. But a deserted cul-de-sac about a mile away had become a quiet and seemingly-safe haven. He would pull in late at night and leave at dawn. He believed no one had noticed the frequent overnight visitor.

He tossed the now-full bag into the truck bed and stood on tiptoe to unlock the driver side door. As he opened the door, he noticed an envelope plastered against the front tire by the wind. He stopped, reached down, and retrieved it. There was no address or stamp. It was sealed but blank.

Curious, he pulled his pocket knife, slipped it under the flap and split the fold. Inside was a Mega Millions lottery ticket. On the third choice down, the numbers were circled in red pen.

Clarence stared at the ticket, his mind not quite comprehending.

"Now why would someone seal a lottery ticket in an envelope? For safe keeping?" he murmured aloud. "No one does that. Unless... maybe they think... or know it's a winner. And the circled numbers? Could they be?"

Clarence looked around nervously, as if expecting someone to run up and instantly claim the envelope and its contents, but there was no one nearby. He quickly climbed into the cab, locked the door, and glanced furtively out every window.

The two power walkers were on the far side of the lake on their second lap. A young family, father pushing a stroller and mother pulling on the arm of an unruly preschooler, were crossing the island bridge. An old man, plastic bag in hand, was picking up after an equally old-looking dog. The park maintenance ground crew was lunching at a table beyond the restrooms. Other than that, no humans were visible. No one had seen him.

Still, Clarence hesitated, unsure what to do.

In the silence of the truck, his brain began to warm to an idea.

*This might be a very lucky day.*

"Okay, Big White Truck, we better check this out," Clarence said as he put the key in the ignition. The truck groaned, sputtered, and died. "Come on, don't quit on me now. I put a buck's worth in you just last week." Again he tried, with the same result. Finally a third try to no avail, except the starter motor grind was beginning to slow.

"Hey Clarence," a voice and loud banging on the passenger side door nearly gave him a heart attack. The older maintenance guy, Carlos, was standing outside. Clarence quickly slipped the ticket into the envelope and stashed it under the driver's seat, and then he leaned over and rolled down the window.

"Having trouble getting her started?" Carlos inquired.

*He didn't see the envelope.* Clarence breathed easier.

"Yeah, think I'm out of gas. She'd sputtered as I pulled into the lot earlier," Clarence said. "Don't relish the trek to the station for a buck's worth, though."

"I got a little left in the mower can. I'll loan you enough to get to the station," Carlos volunteered. Most of the maintenance crew ignored Clarence, but Carlos had always been friendly.

*If this Lotto's a winner*, Clarence thought, *I just might share some with the people like Carlos who've been good to me. Better be careful though; wouldn't want word to get back to Margaret. She'd be after a cut. You can bet on it!*

"Thanks man, I owe you one," Clarence said as Carlos dumped some fuel from a red two-gallon can into the truck's tank before twisting the gas cap back on.

This time, Big White Truck growled, coughed and then sputtered to life. Clarence waved a thank you to the man as he eased her out of the stall and onto the road, remembering to pull the emergency brake to slow down as the brakes took several pumps of the pedal before they would stop the vehicle.

"If this ticket's a winner, I'll get you fixed up," Clarence promised as he patted Big White Truck's dash. "New bakes, shocks, paint job... the works."

He exited the park, made a left at the intersection, thankful that the light was green, and headed into town.

Clarence had never played the Lotto before and didn't know quite what to do or where to go. For a minute he was confused; then he had an idea.

"Seven-Eleven's got a Lotto machine. Bet they can tell me how much I won. Come on Big White Truck, let's head that way."

As he turned down Main toward the store, he was already thinking of ways to spend his winnings, his earlier thoughts of sharing with others forgotten in the euphoria of anticipated wealth.

"First, I'll get some clean clothes and a place to stay. Then a good meal at a fancy, first-class restaurant, one of those places with a *maître d'* and everything. Maybe even do some traveling, see the country. Heck, see the world.

I'll show 'em. I found it and she ain't getting any of it. No way!" He pounded his fist on the steering wheel.

"She don't deserve none of it. None of 'em do. I found it and I'm gonna keep it all."

The sound of a very close air horn shocked Clarence back to reality. He was traveling too fast into the intersection and the light was red. He slammed his foot on the brake. It went to the floor. No slowing. Frantically, he pumped the pedal. Still nothing. The screech of tires caused him to look to the right. Smoke poured from the rear wheels of the sanitation truck that had honked as the driver tried to stop.

Desperately, Clarence jerked the wheel to the left in an effort to avoid and outrun the sanitation truck. The front left wheel of Big White Truck caught the center divider and the vehicle tilted wildly. For an instant, Clarence thought he could save it as he counter-steered to the right but the top-heavy truck had leaned too far and slid onto its side then to its top. The sanitation truck struck and sent Big White Truck careening several hundred feet down the road leaving a trail of bottles, cans, and torn black trash bags.

\*   \*   \*

Officer Philips, first to arrive, took in the scene. Debris littered the street, a dented sanitation truck blocked two lanes, and what had once been a white truck rested on its roof, the cab crushed down to the door handles.

The officer walked around the truck. "Poor bastard," he muttered as it dawned on him that the truck's driver probably didn't survive. He also realized there was little he could do.

Paramedics confirmed the driver probably died instantly. It took several hours to get the vehicles removed and the street cleared.

"It's gonna be another shitty day," Officer Philips murmured. "First the fight with the wife this morning, over money again and now stuck standing out here in the cold while they get this mess cleared up."

As he walked back to the squad car, he noticed they'd missed some trash when sweeping up after the accident, an envelope. He leaned over and picked it up.

"Got to keep the city clean," he remarked as he tossed it into the city-provided recycle bin on the curb.

# Kuniko

Kuniko Ashima folded her parasol, patted her hair to be sure no strands had escaped from her decorative combs, and carefully sat on the park bench in the shade of a large eucalyptus tree to escape the sunlight of the summer day. From there she could see the entire playground.

"*Soko ni itte*, Sarah-chan," she called. Sarah looked up, and Kuniko motioned her four-year-old granddaughter to join the other children. "*Dōzo, dōzo.*"

Sarah's face brightened. "Okay, *Obāchan*," the little girl said with a bow. Then she raced down the hill to join the others on the swings.

*She called me Grandmother!* Kuniko thought. *And her bow was very polite. Keiko has taught her well.*

Kuniko had been staying with her daughter, Keiko, and son-in-law, Gary, since her arrival from Japan seven days earlier. All week, she'd accompanied her daughter and granddaughter on their daily park excursions. Today however, Keiko, who now called herself Kay, had an appointment to translate for several visiting businessmen and asked if *Obāchan* would take Sarah to the park alone. It was only four blocks from their home.

Kuniko watched as Sarah, with hands tightly clenched to the support chains, began to swing. First she kicked her legs forward and let her upper body hang from her hands. The swing moved forward. Then she pulled her shoulders up to meet her hands and tucked her legs under the seat. The swing moved backward. Higher and higher she went with each pass, until Kuniko began to worry that she might fall.

"*Ki o tsukete*, Sarah-chan," she called to the child. *I don't know the English word for 'be careful'*, she thought. *And Sarah doesn't understand* nihongo. *What if something happens? I can't communicate with anyone here.*

Sarah called back, "It's okay. I know what I'm doing."

Of course, her Japanese grandmother didn't understand the English words.

Then Sarah spotted a friend. She quickly brought the swing to a stop and ran to join the other child at the slide. Kuniko exhaled in relief and sat back on the bench.

*What am I doing here?* she thought. *Has it only been six months since Yuki's death? It seems like an eternity. So much has happened.*

Masayuki Ashima, her husband of thirty-five years, had complained of stomach pain and had been hospitalized the previous February. The doctors never told her what was wrong. Every day she took his meals, a change of clothes, and clean bedding to the hospital. Many long hours she sat at the bedside and held his hand. He became weaker and was often sedated. In April, he finally died, and Kuniko was suddenly alone. Following his cremation and internment in the family shrine in *Mikamo,* she officially became a widow.

Yuki had been the leader of the Ashima family on *Shikoku* Island. By custom, their oldest son, Toshihiro, and his wife returned to the family home in *Tokushima* as the new head-of-family. Kuniko was moved from the upstairs master bedroom to the small room next to the kitchen.

She knew well the Japanese saying, "Two women in the household bring bad luck." Kuniko and her daughter-in-law had never gotten along, and the new arrangement strained their relationship even more. When arguments occurred, Toshihiro sided with his wife.

Even worse, Kuniko's married friends no longer came to see her. As a widow, she was now considered *soto*, an outsider, no longer part of the group. She spent long days alone in the room next to the kitchen in the house she and Yuki had shared.

So, when her youngest daughter had invited her mother to visit America, Kuniko, although fearful of going to such a foreign and dangerous place, had accepted.

*After all*, she'd thought, *it may be my only opportunity to see my American grandchild.*

Kuniko had never left *Shikoku* Island before. Now she would travel halfway around the world.

Her son had helped her obtain a passport and travel documents for America and had driven her to the train station for the ride to Osaka. Once on the train, she'd stared out the window at the passing countryside. Rice paddies, small towns, and shiny pachinko parlors had flashed by. Next to her, sat the small suitcase Yuki had used for his business trips to Tokyo. Osaka, even from the train, had looked intimidating.

*So big, so many people*, she'd thought as she exited at *Namba* Station. For a moment, she'd felt like taking the train right back to *Mikamo*. Fortunately, the *Kaisoku*, the rapid-speed train that went direct from the station to *Kansai* airport was at the next platform.

The JAL flight from *Kansai* to Los Angeles International Airport in America had been exciting, but long. She'd never been on an airplane before. The small TV in the seatback ahead of her had shown movies, and announcements had been in both English and *nihongo*.

*Yuki would have loved this. He always wanted to fly.*

Her daughter, Keiko, had been there to greet her at the airport baggage claim with a big American hug, as she called it. In Japan, such public displays were frowned upon.

*There is much to learn about this strange country,* Kuniko had said to herself.

*   *   *

"*Obāchan*, this is my friend Rosie," Sarah said, interrupting Kuniko's thoughts. Next to Sarah was a small, brown-haired, dark-eyed child about her granddaughter's age.

"*Konnichi wa*, Rosie-chan," she said with a respectful bow to the child.

Rosie shyly tangled her fingers in the hem of her shirt and giggled nervously. Behind her stood an elderly lady in a full skirt, white eyelet blouse, and straw hat, who said something to the child in a strange language. Rosie straightened to her full height and said slowly with a practiced voice, "Nice to meet you, Sarah's grandmother."

She looked so serious that both women began to laugh.

The other woman stepped forward, pointed to herself and said, "Carmen Gonzales."

Kuniko made the same gesture, "Kuniko Ashima."

"*Hola*, Kuniko."

"*Konnichi wa*, Carmen-san."

*   *   *

So began the friendship. Each day when Kuniko took Sarah to the park, Carmen and Rosie would be waiting by the playground. While the children played, the two older women sat on the bench, watched the grandchildren, and tried to communicate.

On the third day, Kuniko brought the Japanese-English dictionary Kay had bought for her. It was clean, crisp, and new. Carmen reached into her oversized bag and produced a very dog-eared Spanish-English dictionary.

At first, conversation was very difficult. One would think of something to say and then, using the dictionary, try to translate into English. The hearer would then attempt to translate the English so she could understand. There was much fumbling and hand-gestures between the two women. And when sentences became silly, there was a great deal of laughter.

*     *     *

"Did you know," Kuniko said to her daughter one evening as they sat at the dinner table, "Carmen has four grown children and five grandchildren? The two oldest sons are still living in Juarez. Her daughter and youngest son are here in America. She lives with her daughter and son-in-law and takes care of her granddaughter, too."

"How did you learn all that?" Kay asked. "You only met Carmen a couple of weeks ago."

"Carmen says my English is getting better. She can understand most of what I say."

"All right, say something in English," Kay commanded, crossing her arms in front of herself and looking directly at her mother.

At the first three words, Kay broke into laughter. "You're speaking English with a Spanish accent! I see I'm going to have to give elocution lessons before I have a Japanese mother from south of the border."

*   *   *

For the next three months, Kuniko met Carmen nearly every day and learned not only English, but a little Spanish as well. She also taught Carmen some Japanese. The women were each becoming functional in three languages. The dictionaries were used less, and sentences often began in one language only to finish in another. Each evening, Kay coached her mother in pronouncing English words without the Spanish dialect.

"Will you return to Japan for *Obon*?" Kay asked as they sat following dinner. "Your tourist visa will expire soon."

Kuniko didn't answer.

*I've settled into a comfortable, quiet life here, taking care of Sarah by day, cleaning house, and cooking dinner. It's allowed Kay to take more translation jobs. Gary and Kay seem to want me here. Sarah is the joy of my life. And I've made a friend. Back in Japan, I felt useless. But it is my home.*

"I feel I must go, at least to visit the family shrine and give proper respect to Yuki and the spirits of our ancestors," she said finally with reluctance

The next day at the park, she told Carmen of her decision to return to Japan for *Obon*.

"*Obon*, what is that?"

"It is the *Obon Matsuri*, the festival of lights, the most sacred Buddhist event. We believe the ancestors' spirits come back to their homes to be reunited with their family during *Obon*. I will go to the family shrine and place flowers, fruits, and *chouchin*... in English uh... lanterns, paper lanterns to guide the spirits home. I will pray for Yuki and all the ancestors."

"In Mexico, we have almost the same celebration. It's called *El Día de los Muertos* or 'Day of the Dead.' We pray at the graves of family and friends who have died. We honor the dead by bringing sugar skulls, marigolds, and their favorite foods to the graveside. We even light *luminarias*, paper sacks with candles inside to show the dead the way. How wonderful for you," Carmen said, "to be free to return home. I can only dream of such a thing. But it cannot be."

"Why is that?"

"It is a sad story. I have told no one outside the family. Five years ago, my husband was killed by the drug cartel. It was not safe for me. I paid a *coyote* to transport my youngest son and me to America. The *hombre* took my money and abandoned us in the desert, just this side of the border. We walked two days until we found a city where I was able to call my son-in-law. I am not here legally. I have no passport. If I left, I could not return."

"I'm so sorry," Kuniko said.

That evening she thought about Carmen's story.

*Her life has been so much harder than mine. Yet, she helped me, a total stranger when I first came, and gave me confidence to be with other strangers and not be so afraid. I traveled nine-thousand miles to find a friend.*

\*     \*     \*

The day of Kuniko's departure was approaching. She saw Carmen at the park bench where they had first met.

"*Hola*, Carmen."

"*Konnichi wa*, Kuniko. Have you completed the plans for your trip home?"

"Yes, first I will return to *Mikamo* to pray for Yuki and my family. He left me a nice inheritance, so I will do the things he always talked of, but never did. I will see Tokyo and visit the shrines of Kyoto. See my country. Maybe I'll even climb Mount Fuji. Yuki always wanted to."

Then she added, "Give me the names and address of your sons in Juarez. "I will see if I can visit them on my way back next spring."

"On your way back?"

"Yes, our granddaughters will have finished kindergarten and will need supervision during the summer. And you must know I need to return to see my *saiko tomadachi*, my best friend."

# Wayne

Wayne McIver opened the trunk of his Chevy Cobalt, removed a black box containing a battery-driven portable karaoke machine and spare audio cords. Then he lovingly lifted out his prized Fender Stratocaster. He closed and locked the car, grabbed the box handle, and walked a short distance from the lot to a nearby picnic table in the shade of a large eucalyptus overlooking the lake.

"Perfect," he said with a sigh. "Beautiful clear blue sky and no wind. I don't even need a coat."

Of course, Wayne said the same words most days. It was his routine—some of his co-workers called it a rut—to spend each lunch hour in the park practicing with his guitar.

He flipped opened the latches on the box and placed the karaoke machine on the table. The white stenciled letters on the side had originally read "Mel Ray Music School." Now age had all but obscured the marks.

The Stratocaster looked even more decrepit. Much of the solid body's Lake Placid blue metalflake finish had worn away revealing the older sunburst colors underneath.

Varnish was missing from the rosewood fretboard and the tracks of countless flatpicks had added a rough patina to the pickguard. One of the tone control knobs was missing, but Wayne could still tell its position from the flat side of the remaining post.

Wayne lifted the guitar strap over his head and settled the comfort contour body to its familiar position. He plugged in the cables and switched on the karaoke. It wasn't really an amp. It didn't make much noise. But connecting the guitar to the mike input allowed him to play along with any of a dozen or so cassette tapes of his favorite selections. Besides, it was totally portable, no external power required.

*Well, where should I start?* Wayne thought.

"How about at the beginning?" he said aloud as he reached for his tape of the earliest recordings. He clicked the door shut and pressed play. The first notes started.

Wayne joined in on guitar when the singer began. "When I woke up this morning, you were on my mind..."

Wayne's thoughts flashed back to 1963 and high school.

\*     \*     \*

He was sixteen. He'd received the Stratocaster two years earlier from his father after his mother passed away. He practiced hard and was getting good, or so he believed. One morning, two seniors stopped him between classes.

"Understand you play guitar," the taller one, Mike, said.

"We're putting together a demo tape and need someone who can play lead. You interested?" Jerry added.

Mike and Jerry had a small folk group that performed locally at school dances and the like. Around school they were famous. Why, Mike's older brother John even played with the Kingston Trio. Would he be interested? Of course he'd be interested!

"But I only play electric guitar," he said. "And I don't sing."

"That's okay," Mike explained. "Beverly is our lead singer and the three of us can handle the vocals. We decided electric guitars might be interesting. You know, different from the rest of the acoustic folk groups. We're still hunting for a bass player. Know any?"

"Sorry, can't help you there."

After Don Miller with his electric precision four-string bass joined, they all met to practice three days a week in Mike's Dad's garage. Jerry, Mike, and Beverly soon developed a smooth harmonic blend.

With the basics down, Wayne began improvising. On the last verse of their favorite song, "You Were on My Mind," he toggled the Strat to bright and added a high pitch syncopated rhythm ending in two quick strums. It sounded kind of like, *Tinka-tinka... tinka-tinka... Bring... Bring.*

"Wow, that's good," Jerry exclaimed. "Keep that in."

After a month, the group, still without a name, decided they were ready. Pooling their money, they had just enough to rent a recording studio and an engineer for one night. They cut two songs and sent demos to all the producers they could find.

\*     \*     \*

"A&M wants us," Jerry exclaimed over the phone. "We all have to fly to Frisco to do a real recording Tuesday."

"You're not going," Wayne's father commanded. "No sixteen-year-old son of mine is ditching school and flying to San Francisco."

That was it. The group, minus Wayne, cut the record. It was a huge hit. The house guitarist on the recording even copied Wayne's ending. The band went on tour. Wayne went back to high school. By the time he graduated, the group, now known as *"We Five,"* had already broken up.

Wayne worked as a cashier at McIver's Grocery while attending junior college. He still sat in with local groups whenever possible. One day the phone rang. Jerry, now in Chicago, wanted him for a new band. This was his chance. He packed and flew to Chi-town. It wasn't quite what he'd expected. They did play local clubs on a regular basis, but Wayne found he needed to augment his income by flipping tiny burgers at White Castle. Thousands of tiny burgers.

It did, however, allow him to get to Woodstock and to meet Jimi Hendrix.

Jerry's group didn't have the popularity to command a prime slot. They were relegated to the Sunday, pre-dawn hours. The Woodstock promoters were afraid the four-hundred-thousand attendees would become bored and riot if the music stopped, so groups played through the night.

Wayne had finished a set and was lounging backstage on an overstuffed, ratty sofa, and sharing a joint with the crew, when the military helicopter arrived.

Wayne watched as Jimi unpacked his Stratocaster, the same vintage as his own. But Hendrix's was Buick-pearl-white with a black fingerboard, and left handed.

Jimi muttered, "Time to wake up a half-million people," as he approached the stage. He plugged in, turned up the knobs, raised the pick over his head, and struck downward.

At the first shattering note of "The Star Spangled Banner," Wayne's jaw dropped. No one had ever played like that. Sounds of rockets-red-glare and bombs bursting screamed out over Yasgur's meadow, and beyond.

*"O'er the land of the free... e... e... e... e,"* the clear, super-high pitched note sustained for what seemed an eternity, before *"And the home... of the... Brave."* Hendrix's fingers clamped on the Strat's neck, cutting the sound short. A stunned silence lasted almost thirty seconds before the crowd erupted.

Following the set, Hendrix joined Wayne on the sofa while waiting to be air-lifted out. When Jimi was not stoned, he was quite articulate. They talked guitar.

"See, McIver, the Strats got three pickups," Jimi began. "The bridge pickup has the bright, clean, twangy, sound. The neck pickup is mellower, lower and louder. The middle one is... well... in the middle. The three-position selector switch lets you choose any one pickup. But, if you hold the switch midway between either end and the center position, and jam it with a toothpick or matchstick, you get both pickups active. The string variation over the pair causes a distortion, a tremolo. I call it fuzz."

Wayne noted the matchstick stuck in Jimi's guitar switch.

"More important," Hendrix continued, "this creates feedback that lets you hold the note longer. It's always been the Achilles heel for guitars, no sustain. Sound dies rapidly after the string is plucked. This solves the problem."

Wayne never forgot that conversation.

A year later, Hendrix asked Wayne to join him in England, but by that time McIver had other problems. And then Jimi was dead.

\*     \*     \*

Wayne put in another cassette, grateful for the auto-scan feature that let him quickly locate any song. The tape scanned at high speed until it found a quiet spot, usually between cuts, then stopped and played. Three scans and "Along the Watchtower" began. He performed his best imitation of Hendrix.

*What now?* he thought. *I know, Chicago, "Fancy Colors."* He reached for the tape.

The song always brought the memory of that fateful night.

The guitarist for Chicago had been sick and he'd sat in with the band.

She showed up. Diane. Blond, blue-eyed, eight years his junior. They'd talked between sets. By the time he went back onstage, Wayne knew he was in love. It had taken her a little longer. Ten weeks later, they were married.

Diane and Wayne found an apartment downtown, just inside the loop. Two incomes meant some extra money, and for a few months life was good. Then their lifestyles clashed. She worked days in a bank. He worked nights playing in various clubs around town. They began to drift apart.

Then there was the money thing. Her paycheck was steady; his varied by the number of gigs he took. Wayne's dad always said, "The man brings home the bacon. The wife cooks it." Diane had become the primary breadwinner, and Wayne's ego suffered.

Through the Chicago grapevine, an opportunity to join Carole King's road tour came his way. It offered a chance at real money, but it meant he'd be away from home for three months. He took it.

The tour lasted the three months, then was extended for three more.

Halfway through each performance, Carole would say, "Let's hear it for the band. On lead guitar, we have

Wayne McIver." The spotlight would swing his way and he'd rip a twelve-measure solo on the Strat.

"... and on bass, we have,..." The light would move on.

Wayne was in Alabama when his daughter, Melody, was born. He missed her first steps and first words. He'd written a couple of songs. Carole liked them and said she might use one in the show, but never did. One song, "Rise up Again," was even published in a collection called *Tunes of the Seventies.*

That same year, Wayne's dad died suddenly. Wayne inherited the house in California and decided to move his family there. After all, since he was on the road over two-hundred days a year, it didn't matter where he lived. Diane and Melody would have a real home instead of a crowded apartment.

He was with Bette Midler's world tour when he learned Diane had inoperable breast cancer. He flew home to be with her. Four months later, she died, leaving Wayne with a four-year-old daughter he couldn't relate to. A daughter too young to understand why her mom wasn't there.

The first year was hard. After a disastrous week in Phoenix, stuck with Melody in a hotel room, Wayne realized he couldn't take a five-year-old on tour. She needed a stable home. He'd promised Diane. He realized he'd have to give up the road.

Wayne took a day job as a checker at the local Albertsons, and the Strat went on the shelf. Seven years later, it was still there.

"Daddy," twelve-year-old Melody asked one day, "would you buy me a guitar? Amy has one and is taking lessons. She's my very best friend ever and she said we could start a band, just like 'The Bangles.' Please Dad. Please."

Wayne looked at his daughter. He saw her mother's eyes and long, straight, blonde hair. She was no longer a child, but not yet a woman. Rather, in that gangly in-between stage. But, she was growing up.

"This isn't like that oboe you just had to have for orchestra last year, is it? It's still sitting in your closet." Then he saw the look in her eye and the slight trembling of her chin. He recognized a childhood signal that only occurred when something was very, very important.

"Okay," he said. "Your birthday's coming. If it's what you really want, we can go to the guitar store later today."

"Oh, Daddy, you're the greatest," she exclaimed, giving him a big hug before racing off to tell Amy the good news.

Later that night, after Melody was asleep, her new Ovation acoustic/electric safely stored in its padded case in her closet, Wayne took the Stratocaster from its home on the top shelf and borrowed his daughter's new practice mini-amp. He hadn't touched the Strat in seven years.

He tuned it. The strings were dead, but otherwise the pickups and controls worked fine. He played quietly for several minutes. In the middle of the intro to "Stairway to Heaven," he saw Melody standing in the doorway.

"Daddy... keep playing," she said. "Until I heard the music, I'd forgotten. You played guitar before Mama died. It was so long ago. Did you stop on account of me?"

He saw the slight tremble of her lower lip.

"No, Mel, it was time. I needed to get some priorities straight. You were only part of it. Besides, I wouldn't have missed watching you grow up for anything."

He was rewarded by the smile on his daughter's face. "Say, could you show me some of those fancy things you were doing? They sounded really cool." She plopped down on the sofa next to him.

\*     \*     \*

26

As Wayne finished playing "Manic Monday" and pulled the cassette from the machine, he remembered when Melody had tried to learn it.

She and Amy had taken professional lessons. The instructor was thrilled by how fast they'd progressed. "My best students," he'd often repeat. He didn't know Wayne often sat in with the girls when they were practicing, filling in the background while they worked from the sheet music.

One evening while doing dinner dishes, Melody said, "Dad, I talked to Matt Jones at school today. His father's starting a band and needs a guitarist." She handed him a plate to dry and continued, "You should do it."

"Mel, I don't do any of the new music, and haven't really practiced for years."

"Dad, Matt says it's going to be a sixties rock band. Matt complains all his dad ever plays is the 'old stuff.' You'd fit right in. Please, Daddy, for me."

"Okay, I'll talk to Matt's father, but no promises. I still have a store to manage, after all."

\*     \*     \*

"You're Wayne McIver? *The* Wayne McIver?" Bob Jones had asked when they met in Bob's garage. "When Matt told me a classmate's father played guitar, I didn't connect the name, until now."

"It's been a long time. Maybe you should hear me first."

"Okay, try this one," Bob said as he pulled some worn sheet music from a pile. "It's called 'Rise up Again' by somebody named Wayne McIver. The chording is a little sparse. I've always wondered what it should really sound like."

\*     \*     \*

A light afternoon breeze rustled the leaves of the eucalyptus and raised a small cloud of dust from the park's path as Wayne played the last chords of "Rise up Again."

*Hard to believe the band Bob and I started over twenty years ago is still going strong. Of course now they're called 'tribute bands' and are all the rage. Got two gigs lined up for the weekend. Who'd have thought?*

He looked at his watch, unplugged the Strat, and began to pack.

*Better head for home. Melody and the grandkids will be over later today. Chuck will want the charcoal hot in my Weber when he comes from work. He and I promised to fix dinner for the family tonight.*

# Jenny

"Theodore Thornton Junior, be careful where you're going!" Jenny shouted as the six year old on his electric 'Big Foot' off-road four-wheeler scattered a group of ducks from the lakefront path and crashed into a bush in the process. *Why did I ever let your father talk me into allowing him buy such a dangerous toy?*

She knew the reason. It was her husband's special gift to his son, knowing he wouldn't be around for the boy's seventh birthday. Surgeon Major Theodore Thornton was midway through his third rotation in Afghanistan and would not return home for another seven months.

Teddy looked up, flashed the impish smile he always used when he'd done something a bit naughty. And after backing out of the bush that had entangled the left front wheel, he slipped the stick shift into forward, slammed the accelerator to the floor, and raced straight down the long, steep, grass-covered hill toward the empty soccer field and lower parking area.

The first time Teddy had aimed the car down the steep incline, Jenny had panicked.

But her husband held her back. "Just watch him," he'd said. "I taught him to handle the hill. He'll be fine."

Little Teddy had returned, all smiles, to the praises of his dad.

She watched her son slow the electric vehicle at the bottom, turn, and start toward the winding asphalt path that lead back to the top. The little car could move quickly downhill, but the small electric motor couldn't negotiate the steep, grassy climb. She would have several minutes of peace while her son took the long pathway back.

Jenny sighed. *You're more like your father every day: rebellious and headstrong. You have to do everything your own way. Yes, just like your father.*

She remembered that day eight years before. They'd only been married for four months. Ted had come home from his college class, excited about a way to achieve his lifelong dream of becoming a pediatric surgeon.

"Honey," he declared, "the recruiter said my grades are good enough. I could join the Air Force and qualify for the Health Professional Scholarship Program. It means my education and medical training would all be paid for by the federal government. I could graduate from medical school debt free."

"And, what does the government get for all this?" she questioned.

"After I finish, I become a second lieutenant in the Air Force and serve four years of active duty. But it's a great opportunity. Desert Storm is over, and we're at peace. I don't think we'll get into another war so soon."

At the time, she thought so too, and reluctantly agreed. Of course, that was before 9-11, Afghanistan, Operation Iraqi Freedom, and the ongoing conflict.

$*$   $*$   $*$

Jenny watched her son continue his slow drive to the top. While seated at the bench on the hilltop, she thumbed through the mail she'd picked up on the way to the park. Under the bills and store flyers, she discovered the letter from Tom.

*Why didn't I see this before?* She hurriedly opened it.

*Air Force Theater Hospital, Afghanistan*
*Thursday, 3 April*

*Dearest Jenny,*

> *As I sit in my hooch, it's about midnight here. I find it hard to believe I'm only half way through my deployment. Time is not constant in Afghanistan, it speeds by or it crawls, often in the same day. Or maybe I'm more aware. I've just come off a twenty-four-hour shift.*
> *Tonight brought home just how much I miss you and Teddy. There was an alarm red around seventeen-hundred on Tuesday. I was at the surgeons' call building when we heard the blast. Surgeon Cliff, physician assistant Julie, and I went to the top of the building. Looking out over the stacked sandbags, we could see smoke rising from beyond the palm trees outside the wire. I prayed no one was hurt.*
> *Fifteen minutes later, my pager went off. I donned my helmet and Kevlar vest and headed for the ER. We're required to wear armor during an alarm red. As I approached the building, one Black Hawk helicopter had already landed and another was approaching for dust-off. The first of the injured began to*

*arrive, three American soldiers and several Afghan police officers. Commander Scott triaged the incoming and made assignments. Surgeon Cliff took the first soldier, I the second. The nurses and techs had already prepped him and started an intravenous catheter. Their Humvee had hit an improvised explosive device (IED). My patient's left leg was peppered with shrapnel. We cleaned the wounds, stabilized the broken leg, and applied antibiotics and dressings to ease the pain. Patched up and prepped, the Americans were evacuated by the critical air transport team (CATT) to Germany. Locals were also patched up, but were sent to an uncertain fate in Afghan hospitals. Those hospitals are understaffed and short on supplies. I pray those men will continue to recover.*

*It was about nineteen-thirty when I changed out of bloody scrubs and donned armor for the short walk home and to bed. I didn't make it. My pager sounded again.*

*A young Afghan boy, about Teddy's age, was brought in, another victim of the same violence. His family had taken him to a local hospital, but his injuries were more than they could treat, so they sent him here. With the alarm red, the family was not allowed on base. Only the father was let in with the boy. Being the only pediatric surgeon on staff, I was given this new charge. Surgeon Cliff and I worked several hours to stabilize him. His injuries were severe. Shrapnel wounds to the torso, head, and left arm. The worst was that he'd lost a lot of blood and was not breathing on arrival. As you know, the first thirty minutes after an incident are the most critical. Perhaps if I'd seen him sooner...*

*The EKG results showed minimal brain activity. We put him on a ventilator. I set up an around-the-clock nursing team to monitor the child. The father refused to leave and was given a cot next to his son.*

*For two days, we watched for any sign of improvement. The father stayed resolutely near his son, Touma. Several times, nurses returning from the hospital DFAC, brought MREs to share with the man.*

*Finally, the team came to the realization that we couldn't save the child. The damage to his head and brain was too great. There was nothing more we could do for him here, and he'd never survive a flight to Germany or the US. If he managed to make it, he'd probably remain in a vegetative state.*

*The translator and I met with the father. A conversation I dreaded. I explained the situation. The translator cried; the father cried; I cried. Finally, he agreed to let us remove the ventilator and thanked us for the care we'd given his son. Touma died twenty minutes later in his dad's arms.*

*We cleaned and wrapped the body in pads and a blanket. Then CATT Sergeant Doug commandeered a Humvee to drive the boy and his father to the front gate where the family we'd notified by phone waited.*

*He was not the first child who died here. Nor do I delude myself that he will be the last. Tomorrow I'll go back to the ER and help others who may come my way. But for tonight, I am desolate.*

*I miss you and cannot wait till I can hold both you and Teddy in my arms again. Till then, I hold you in my prayers.*

*All my love,*
*Ted*

\*    \*    \*

Tears dripped onto the letter as she finished reading.

"Mommy, why are you crying?" Teddy's voice sounded scared and his blue eyes, so like his father's, looked up into hers.

"I was just reading a letter from Daddy, and it made me sad. He misses you and me so much and would love to come home, but he has very important work to finish."

"I miss my daddy." The child's lip quivered. "Will he come home soon?"

"Not in time for your birthday, I'm afraid. But he'll be back before Christmas."

"Oh." The boy paused. "But that's a long time."

"I know, Teddy, and I'm sure it makes Daddy very sad to be away. Maybe we can cheer him up. Why don't we go home and write him a letter. You can tell him all about school and first grade and how much fun it is to drive your own car around the park. I'll bet that will make him happy."

The boy's expression brightened.

"Okay," he said. "Race you to the car." He again turned the four-wheeler and sped down the hill toward the parking lot and waiting minivan.

*Yes, just like his father*, she thought, shaking her head as she rose from the bench to follow her son.

# Carol

Carol Cooper always knew what she wanted to be when she grew up. Of course, it changed every few years. When she was seven, she was going to be a princess and live in a castle at Disneyland. By age eleven, she expected her letter from Hogwarts to attend wizarding classes. Then in high school she discovered writing.

In college she excelled in both English and journalism. During her junior year, she won a coveted position on the official campus newspaper, *The Daily Oracle*. As the newest staff member, she wrote several columns on student activities, but nothing very interesting. She longed for an important assignment. So when her editor called her in, she was excited.

"Carol, I'd like you to do a piece for the Arts and Music section," he explained. "The college is dedicating the new music wing to Dr. James Mueller. Our staff files don't have any information about him since his retirement. I'd like you to interview him. You know, one of those 'Where are they now?' stories." He handed her a folder.

Back at her desk, she opened the file. Dr. Mueller had an impressive record: accomplished musician, graduate of the prestigious Julliard School of Music, founder and first director of the OC Symphony, composer, and published author.

*This could be a great interview. It says here he retired as head of the college music department at sixty-five. But that was thirteen years ago. He would be seventy-eight now. There's no obituary, so he must still be alive.*

She tried online for a phone number, but found none. *Maybe it's unlisted. Well, I have his last known address. It's close by. I'll go there this afternoon.*

* * *

Carol drove slowly along the quiet residential street looking for the address. Tall oak trees on each side overhung the roadway, casting patterns of dark and light on the cracked and worn pavement. The shadows made reading the faded and chipped addresses painted on the curbs difficult. She reached the far end and still hadn't found the right house number.

*These old neighborhoods sure don't make it easy. Guess I'll have to get out and walk.*

Carol parked and locked the car. Then, on foot, she retraced her path down the street. Walking along, she peered at each house, looking to match a name or number. Several of the residences were well-maintained. Others showed neglect. Many were hidden by fences or overgrown shrubbery. All were old. Finally she saw a mailbox with the address matching the file.

*This must be the place.*

Behind a brick wall, partially covered in vines, a small 1920s vintage shingled cottage sat far back on a large lot. A winding flagstone path led from the ornate wrought-iron gate to the front porch.

"Hello," Carol called several times. "Is anybody home?" But there was no answer. She tried the gate. It wasn't locked. The hinges creaked as she pushed it open.

In several places along the path, tree roots had lifted and cracked the flagstones. Soft daylight filtered through the overhanging canopy of tree limbs and leaves and cast a gray pallor over the uneven path.

*I'd sure hate to attempt this at night.*

As she approached the cottage, she noted its foundation was made of large round boulders stacked and grouted together. Columns of the same material supported the corners of the porch roof and bracketed the stairs leading to the front door. The center tread creaked in protest as she climbed the three steps to the wooden porch.

*No doorbell. Oh, but there's a brass knocker.* After opening the outer screen door, she rapped three times.

"Just a moment," a pleasant-sounding female voice answered from inside. The door opened a few inches to reveal a slightly stooped elderly woman. Her long gray hair was pulled into a ponytail.

"May I help you?" she asked.

"I'm from the college newspaper," Carol said holding out her ID. "Does Professor James Mueller live here?"

"Why, yes dear, he does. I'm Marian, his wife. I assume you're here because of the dedication. We have so few visitors these days. Won't you please come inside?" She unhooked the chain.

Carol followed her into a small but tidy front room. An overstuffed sofa, armchair, and floor lamp, reminiscent of an earlier era, were at one end. A rock fireplace filled the other. Through a pillared archway, she could see a dining room with built-in glass-door cabinets displaying china plates and crystal goblets.

"This way, dear," Marian said, leading her through a side door into the kitchen. She pointed to a chrome dinette set. "Please be seated. Would you like some tea?" She struck a match and lit a burner beneath a kettle on the stove.

"That would be lovely, thank you," Carol said. "Is your husband home? I'd like to interview him."

The old lady's smile melted into a sad expression. "Yes, he's here. But he's not giving interviews anymore. You see, my husband of fifty-three years was diagnosed with Alzheimer's several years ago. The disease has robbed him of many memories. He no longer recalls when he was a star student, Julliard graduate or symphony conductor. As an author, he wrote textbooks describing folk music from around the world. Now that world has shrunk to this house where he grew up and our walks around the neighborhood. Most of the day, James spends his time trying to assemble the jigsaw puzzles I put out."

"Oh, I'm so sorry."

"Don't be sad for us, dear. James's spirit is still inside him. He still says, 'Good morning, darling,' and kisses me each day when we wake up. That's all I need."

Marian glanced at the clock on the kitchen wall. "My, look at the time, almost four o'clock. James and I must take our afternoon walk. We'd be pleased if you'd join us."

Returning to the living room, Marian retrieved a cane and paused at the entrance to a small study. Inside Carol saw a man seated in a recliner peering out a window to the rear yard, his back to the door.

"Come, James," Marian called. "It's time for our constitutional."

James immediately rose to his feet, started toward the door, and smiled. His pale blue eyes crinkled at the corners as he focused on his wife. To Carol, he appeared to be lean and fit, if a bit stooped.

Marian leaned on her cane for support as she and Carol waited. After James joined them on the porch, Marian closed and locked the house.

Marian told him, "This is Ms. Cooper. She's joining us today."

James said, "Hello, Ms. Cooper," and held out his hand. The shake was firm and friendly.

"Take my arm, dear," Marian said.

Carol followed as, arm-in-arm, the couple walked the front path, through the wrought-iron gate to the sidewalk and street beyond.

A late fall afternoon breeze fluttered the leaves on the branches of the scrub oak and eucalyptus that bordered the walkway. At the corner, the threesome turned toward the park. Cars and trucks whizzed by on the street, their occupants taking no interest in Carol or the elderly couple.

As they approached the entrance to Lakeview Park, one of the gardeners cut the engine of his riding mower and waved to them.

"Afternoon Marian, James," the man called across the low hedge that separated the park proper from the public sidewalk. "Who's your friend?"

"Hello, Carlos. This is Carol Cooper. She's doing an interview on James for the college newspaper," Marian called back. James nodded.

As they neared the park entrance, the sidewalk split. The path to the left led into the park; the other headed on toward Main Street and the shopping center. James started to the right.

Marian gently reminded him "Park, honey... We'll do our shopping tomorrow."

He smiled and turned onto the left-hand pathway.

"Must be four o'clock," Carlos announced as they approached. "I can pretty well set my watch by when you arrive each day."

"Well, James likes to keep to a routine," Marian admitted.

"Do you know the Muellers well?" Carol asked Carlos.

"Sure do," Carlos said. "They've been walking around the lake for as long as I can remember. They used to do three laps every day, but Marian's hip's been bothering her lately and she can't keep up with James anymore. I get off work about now, so I walk with 'em. That way, James has company, and Marian, when she gets tired, can find a bench and wait for us to come around again."

"Okay if I join you?" Carol asked.

"Sure, if you can keep up. James sets a mean pace and don't take kindly to 'slackers', as he calls 'em, you know, those people that just meander along. Sometimes I even have trouble keeping up."

James stood at the edge of the path overlooking the lake, his arms clasped behind his back, eyes slowly scanning the expanse of water, his gaze pausing occasionally to study a group of ducks or other water fowl.

Finally he turned to Carlos. "Looks good," he commented. "Won't need to add water."

"Yeah, level's up full," Carlos answered. Then he leaned toward Carol, placed his hand beside his mouth and said in a voice only she could hear, "He says that every day. I think he remembers when they drained the lake to build the park. He must have been a kid. That was a long time ago, before I started here, and it seems like

I've been here forever." Then in a louder voice he said, "Ready for your walk, James? We'll just follow the path today. Why don't you take the lead?"

James smiled back and set off at a crisp pace. The others followed. Soon Marian slowed and stopped at the first bench. James pushed on ahead.

Carol and Carlos trailed a few yards behind.

"It's nice of you to do this for the Muellers," Carol said.

"Well, I've known them a long time. Before James's illness, he was one of the nicest, humblest people you'd ever meet, always helping others. Marian's no slouch either. You know, she was a noted anthropologist and former university professor. Now she spends all her time as his caregiver. Anything I can do to help, I will."

*        *        *

"Come sit by me," Marian called as James passed on his third lap. He stopped and joined her on the bench. They held hands as the sun dropped behind the trees and up-lit the clouds to a bright, slowly-fading, red-orange glow.

Carlos excused himself to leave for home and dinner. Carol settled next to the couple.

"Isn't it beautiful?... The... the..." James stammered looking for a word he intuitively knew but the disease had robbed him of.

"Sunset," Marian suggested.

His neurons finally found the connection. "Yes! Sunset. I think it's time we went home, dear," he said, rising and taking her hand to help her up.

Carol watched as the couple walked away arm-in-arm in the growing darkness.

*Certainly a far different story than I'd anticipated. I know what I'm going to write about, though. Even through the worst of times, this couple's love survives. I pray they have many more "Good morning, darling" days.*

# Shirley

"Where is that caterer?" Shirley Lockhart could feel the tension rising inside her. "He was supposed to be here at ten-thirty and it's almost eleven.  People will start arriving for the company picnic around eleven-thirty, and there's no food yet."

Kristen, her best friend and company cohort, looked up from placing the last of the spring flower centerpieces on the twenty or so tables in covered picnic area number two. "It'll be all right, you'll see," she said.

"Why did I ever agree to plan this shindig?" Shirley muttered to herself. "I've only been with Precision Performance eighteen months. It's not fair. Where's my help?"

The planning had been more difficult than she'd ever expected. Her boss, Mark Pendleton, had asked her to organize the company picnic last March, just three months before. Shirley would do anything for him, even that.

Truth be told, she'd had a crush on the Marvelous Mr. Pendleton since the first time they met on her second day at work. He was tanned and tall with an athletic build.

She secretly suspected that under the white shirt and tie, he had a flat stomach and solid abs. After all, he'd just turned thirty, only four years older than she.

To be named as his executive assistant after only seven months might have seemed like the luckiest of coincidences, but it had taken a lot of effort, extra hours, and volunteering for several special projects to land the coveted spot. At first Mark had been the perfect gentleman and boss, complementing her good work, always friendly and courteous. She secretly wanted much more. The only one who knew about her feelings for Mr. Wonderful was Kristen.

When Mark had suggested the picnic, she'd eagerly agreed. If the picnic was a success, it would insure her position and maybe, just maybe, Mark would really look her way.

Now, she had second thoughts. Marvelous Mark had all but abandoned her. He hadn't been in his office in several weeks and only spoke to her by phone occasionally. The picnic became her responsibility. There had been reservations to make, menus to select, a catered meal for one-hundred twenty-five people, and a Mariachi band to hire. If it hadn't been for Kristen, she'd never have been ready.

"I'll nail this to the main entry gate," Kristen said. She picked up the hand-lettered pasteboard sign, complete with painted company logo, and four helium-filled party balloons. She also grabbed the staple-gun and started toward the entrance. "No one will be able to miss these directions."

"Kristen, you're a lifesaver," Shirley said.

"You'd better contact the caterer. Find out what's holding him up," Kristen called as she lugged the sign up the path. "At least we won't be thirsty," she said passing the row of ice chests containing soft drinks, iced tea, and bottled water. Park rules forbade alcoholic beverages.

"Right," Shirley agreed, taking out her cell phone. She keyed in the number.

"Kinoshita Catering... heh-row," a female voice answered. Shirley suspected from the accent, English was not her first language.

"Mr. Kinoshita, please."

"He no here now."

"Can you tell me where he is?"

"He no here now, lunchtime—work."

"He's supposed to be catering the Precision Performance picnic lunch today. Is he on his way?"

The woman answered a little louder. "He no here now. You call later, okay?"

Shirley's voice rose. "Not okay. Tell Mr. Kinoshita to call Shirley Lockhart right away!"

The voice on the other end sounded close to tears. "He no here now, lunchtime—work. You call later, okay?"

Shirley realized she had probably heard the extent of the woman's English vocabulary and figured further conversation was useless. Fortunately, a large white step-van with the words "Kinoshita Catering" in big red letters on the side had just entered the parking lot.

Using her most soothing tone, she said, "Okay, I'll call later," and hung up.

Mr. Kinoshita and two very young Asian girls, each wearing white starched butcher coats, paper hats, and blue jeans, sprang from the van and began to unload equipment.

Mr. Kinoshita, out of breath as he wheeled one of two big hibachi barbeques up the path near where Shirley stood, stopped and made a quick bow.

"So sorry, Ms. Lockhart. Truck got lost in traffic. But we ready quick. Food much good. You like, I promise," he said with a second bow.

\*     \*     \*

Twelve noon. Shirley stood atop the concrete ring surrounding the empty fire pit to get a better overview of the area. Everything seemed to be going well. Mariachi music filled the air as the costumed musicians went from table to table singing and taking requests. Mr. Kinoshita and his crew were keeping the buffet tables filled. Shirley's menu choice of strip steaks, ribs, and barbequed chicken, instead of the hamburger and hot-dogs of previous years, was a definite hit. And the salad bar with rice, mixed greens, sliced fresh fruit, and ambrosia, beat out warm potato salad any day.

"This is one great picnic," announced Ron from Accounting as he passed by with his second, or maybe his third plate.

*This is almost perfect,* Shirley thought, *except for one thing.*

At that moment, Kristen stepped next to her and whispered, "So where's Prince Charming? I thought Cinderella was supposed to make the late entrance, not the prince."

"He'll be here. Mark called this morning, said he could be a little late, and that he might have a surprise."

Kristen leaned closer. "If the past two weeks are any indication, I'd say the surprise would be if Mister 'You can count on me' shows up at all. Aren't you the least bit angry with him?"

"He must have a good reason," Shirley replied.

*I'm not sure whether I'm really angry, or just hurt,* Shirley thought. *It's not like Mark to be mean. I just hope he can explain when he gets here. Where is he?*

\*     \*     \*

Lunch was almost over. Mr. Connor, the CEO, was finishing his meal and would soon make his annual speech.

*Where is Mark?*

Finally, Shirley saw Mark's gray BMW pull into the parking lot. Her eyes followed as the car found an empty stall. Mark stepped out and adjusted his tie. Then he walked to the passenger side, opened the door, and reached in to assist the occupant. Out stepped this... this blonde. She was tall, maybe five-foot ten, and looked to be in her mid-twenties.

"Oh no, a song leader," Shirley murmured. *Where did that come from? I haven't thought about that description since graduation.*

In her sorority at UCI, females had come in two types, cheerleaders and song leaders. Shirley had been the former, short, tom-boyish, and athletic. Guys were "buddies" or friends. Cheerleaders wore oversize sweatshirts, shorts, and tennis shoes. Song leaders, on the other hand, wore fringed bolero vests over blouses tied in front, pleated short skirts, white boots, waved pom-poms, and went on serious dates. This one was definitely song leader.

The two walked up the path arm-in-arm, smiling and talking.

"Would you look at that," Kristen declared. Then she snickered and whispered to her friend, "Bet that's an expensive arm decoration."

Shirley felt sick.

Mark and the blonde, stopped to talk to Mr. Connor. They were too far away and the band too loud for her to hear any of the conversation.

*They're headed this way.* Mark had spotted her in the crowd and was moving directly toward her, blonde in tow.

"Shirley, congratulations. Connor tells me this is the best company picnic ever. I knew you'd come through." Mark gestured toward the lady clinging to him. "Shirley, this is Taylor Thompson. Taylor, meet Shirley Lockhart, the best executive assistant in the entire company."

"Pleased to meet you, Ms. Lockhart. Markie's told me so... much about you. I feel I know you already." Her soft soprano voice was a combination of mint julep and warm honey with a breathiness that screamed 'Southern Belle.'

"Can I get you anything, Taylor?" Mark asked, pointing to the buffet.

"No food, honeybunch. Lunch at Summit House was superb." She paused. "I could use a drink. None of that soft sarsaparilla, though. There's some white zinfandel in my briefcase. Perhaps you could get it from your car, shugah. You think anyone would object if you filled one of those paper cups for little ole me?"

At that moment, Mr. Connor rose from his seat, tapped a plastic knife on his empty coke can, and called for attention. Conversation stopped.

"Employees, guests, and friends of Precision Performance welcome. Even with the economy, this has been a good year for P-cubed, and we have all of you to thank for our success. Our prospects for next year are even better. I'm proud to announce that, following extensive negotiations, we've signed an agreement with Thompson Enterprises. Discussions were kept secret until the merger was finalized to avoid affecting stock prices, but this joining of companies will prove beneficial to both our firms. I would like to especially thank Mark Pendleton for his work above and beyond the call of duty. Mark, bring Ms. Thompson up here. Everyone, this is Taylor Thompson, President of Thompson Enterprises. Let's have a round of applause..."

\*  \*  \*

Most of the others had left. The Mariachis had packed their instruments and Mr. Kinoshita was loading his step-van. Mark separated from Mr. Connor and Ms. Thompson, who was still sipping her forbidden white wine, and walked to where Kristen and Shirley were standing, glaring at him.

"Don't let him off the hook too easy," Kristen whispered in Shirley's ear, as she left her and walked toward Mark.

"You better be nice," Kristen said to him as she passed. "While you were out... entertaining, she saved your event, you know." She continued toward the parking lot leaving the two alone.

Mark watched her go and then turned to Shirley.

"I'm sorry," he said. "It was wrong of me to have dumped all the party preparation on you, but Mr. Connor didn't give me any choice. The merger took priority over everything else. Plus, it was all hush-hush. I couldn't tell anyone, not even my favorite executive assistant."

"I must say, I was upset when you didn't help like you said you would. Then you were late, and when you finally arrived you showed up with her! What's a girl to think?"

"You're right. Can I make it up to you? How about dinner Friday night? I know a great little Italian place. Say seven-thirty?"

"Well, I'll have to think..." Inside her mind was screaming. *Don't let this go by. It's what you wanted, isn't it? Tell him!*

"Yes, Yes I'd like to go, but what about... you know." Shirley gestured with a tilt of her head.

"Taylor? She's a very interesting woman. She puts on a great act, but under the dumb blonde persona, there's a very savvy businesswoman. Anyway, she's Connor's problem now. It'll be just the two of us, I promise."

Shirley was sure the smile on Mark's face was matched only by her own. *This was the best picnic ever, and it's only the beginning.*

# Alex

Alex cringed as the high-pitched whine of the tiny engine on the radio-controlled off-road 4x4 model racer shattered the park's calm. Looking up, he spotted a telltale dust trail as the model car streaked across the dirt lot, headed for the fire pits. It rounded the far trees, cut across the walking path, and scattered a family of ducks before it struck a fallen log, flipped into the air, and landed wheels up.

"Damn youngsters," Alex muttered as he spotted the three boys, probably junior-high age he guessed, as they emerged laughing from behind the nearby stand of eucalyptus.

"Don't you know the rules?" he called. "Sign says no gas-powered toys allowed in the park."

"Easy, old man," the one in dirty cutoff jeans and carrying the pistol-grip R/C controller called back. "We'll be gone long before the cops can get here." A second boy set the idling vehicle upright on its wheels.

With a twist on the controller and a, "See ya later, granddad," from its operator, the 4x4 sprang to life, hung several donuts in the dirt field, then headed around the south end of the lake, the three youth in pursuit.

*Granddad? Indeed!* thought Alex after they'd disappeared. Although old enough to have grandkids, Alex and Eileen, his wife of nearly fifty years, had never had, would never have, children. Sadness crossed his mind like a small cloud on an otherwise sunny day.

"Hey, today's Wednesday. Best day of the week! Can't be sad on a Wednesday," Alex intoned as he turned back to unload his '94 Buick Roadmaster Estate Wagon. "The rest of the guys should show up any time now."

For Alex, Wednesday was the best day. Once a week, the R/C sailboat club met to practice at Lakeview Park. This day Alex was dressed in his finest sailing attire: white milkman pants, matching white nylon jacquard shirt, and deck shoes. A blue ascot and classic Panama hat topped off the outfit. "Spiffy," Eileen had once called the ensemble.

First, Alex retrieved the wooden carryall and set it on its wheels behind the car. Then he carefully slid his prized Chesapeake racing sloop, The Eileen II, from the rear of the Buick and strapped it to the specially-built carrier. As he straightened up, Alex's hand pressed into the small of his back to ease the stiffness of the arthritis. *Pain's not too bad today.*

He hung the twin joystick-control unit on a lanyard about his neck and pushed the walker that doubled as his chair. Then Alex slowly towed the model sailboat down the asphalt path to the small peninsula that protruded into the lower lake.

*The others should be along anytime,* he thought as he glanced at his watch. *Guess they're running a little late.*

A light wind rippled the waters. A few fluffy clouds dotted the horizon. Overhead nothing but blue sky. Perfect weather for sailing.

"Where are they?" he muttered. "I really need to see them, especially today." Will and Pete were always on time. Besides, someone had to help him get the sailboat into and out of the water. It was a task he could no longer do alone. Alex parked the boat carrier near the water's edge, lowered the seat on his walker and settled in to wait for the others.

As Alex sat alone on the peninsula, last Friday replayed in his memory like an endless tape.

\*     \*     \*

He'd fed Eileen lunch at the nursing home as he had nearly every meal the past three years. The morphine patches that eased her pain had also robbed the sparkle from her eyes and the smile from her lips.

In the first years, she had often asked, "Why is God keeping me here? He must know I'm ready."

Alex had no answer.

Now she spoke only with her eyes. Her voice silent.

Alex pushed the button to raise the hospital bed to a feeding position but Eileen slumped to the left, and he no longer had the strength to straighten her.

*No nurse around. I'll just have to make do.*

*Vegetable soup, her favorite*, he thought as he stirred the contents of the bowl. He carefully scooped a half teaspoon of broth and vegetables.

*Not too much now, wouldn't want her to choke.* Eileen's mouth opened automatically as the spoon neared her lower lip.

"Would you like some carrots and mashed potatoes?" he asked. "The gravy sure looks good." Alex carefully avoided today's main dish, jambalaya, knowing it was not a favorite. Even so, her mouth refused to open. Soup was all she'd take.

"How about a little Ensure then?" he asked as he lifted the container and placed the straw between her lips. Slowly, the white liquid rose in the straw as if the effort needed to suck in the nourishment was almost beyond Eileen's strength. After a minute, the straw slipped from her mouth. Alex used the terrycloth bib to wipe her lips and chin.

Then he talked: about any news he heard, church activities, the neighbors who asked her about her condition, the garden, whatever would break the silence.

"The Double Delight and Mr. Lincoln in the front yard are both blooming right now. I'll bring you a rose bouquet tonight when I come for dinner. Would you like that?" No response. "But your poor Marilyn Monroe's been attacked by aphids. I sprayed it this morning and I'm hopeful it'll recover." The vacant eyes shifted his way and he sensed a spark of life behind them.

When the talking was done, he sat and held her hand. The once-soft, smooth skin was now tissue thin and almost transparent, revealing the blood vessels and bones underneath.

During their long silence, her shallow breathing stopped. Alex felt the pressure of her hand release. He rose and kissed her a last time.

Alex pressed the nurse call button. There was no panic, no rush to supply air or restart her heart. Her instructions had been clear: no resuscitation. The nurse entered, followed by Kathy from hospice.

Most of the paperwork had been completed beforehand; just a release was left to sign.

Alex retrieved his walker and started toward to the side entrance and the parking lot to await the coroner, but Kathy stopped him.

"Here at Lakeside Extended Care," she declared, "the deceased go out with dignity by the front door, accompanied by their loved ones."

Two orderlies arrived and carefully lifted Eileen onto the gurney. They arranged her on her back, arms at her side, and placed a white sheet over her body.

*She looks so peaceful, just as if she's asleep.*

With Kathy on one side and a nurse on the other, Alex followed the slow procession down the hallway to the main entrance.

"*Amazing grace how sweet the sound...,*" Kathy sang softly. Staff members appeared in the doorways along the corridor. Other voices joined the song, "*... T'was blind, but now I see.*"

Alex, always stoic, hadn't broken down until safely in the privacy of the old Buick. He gripped the steering wheel till his arms and knuckles hurt. And he cried. A long time later, after the tears subsided, he drove home, only to begin again, alone in the dark and quiet of his empty house.

\*     \*     \*

"Hey old man, you just gonna sit there?"

A startled Alex raised his head and found himself on the peninsula, still waiting. He looked for the source of the voice. The young boy he'd seen earlier, in the same cutoff jeans and dirty tee-shirt, was sitting on the knoll behind the little point of land.

"They ain't coming today, yah know," the boy said getting to his feet. "Heard you all talking last week bout some big contest or something."

"The AMYA regatta at City Park," Alex exclaimed. "I was supposed to be there."

"That a big deal?" The boy asked.

"The American Model Yachting Association annual regatta, you bet it is." Alex put his hand to his forehead. "How could I have forgotten?"

*Silly old man, you'll catch a ribbing for this one. The guys will tag you with the Geezer of the Month award for sure.*

Alex looked at the boy on the shore. "How'd you know about the regatta? I don't remember seeing you before today."

"I'm here every week. You guys get so hooked on your boat races that a fire truck could park here and you wouldn't notice. You going to sail today? Or what?"

"I need help getting the sloop into and out of the water. You want to give me a hand?"

"Sure, old man, got nothing else to do," he said as he came forward.

"Got a name, son? Mine's Alex."

"Dennis."

"Nice to meet you, Dennis." Alex held out his hand and the boy timidly accepted his grasp.

Together they lowered the craft into the lake. Alex picked up the controller, slid into his chair and adjusted the levers to head the sloop toward the first of four marker buoys. Actually, they were just floats with flags on top the club had anchored to the lake bottom to create a closed sailing course.

"Can you make it go any faster?" asked Dennis.

"This isn't like that hot-wheel you had earlier. This craft takes finesse and knowledge of wind and water. By the way, what happened to your friends?"

Dennis shrugged. "Oh, Robby had to take his off-roader car home. He wasn't too happy with me for flippin' it. Evan went with him."

The sloop rounded the first flag. "Now you'll see some speed," Alex said as he pushed the stick to tighten the sail. The little craft heeled over and accelerated.

"Wow, she can really move. I learned in class that sailboats are always shes," Dennis said proudly.

"You want to try her?" Alex said handing over the console.

"Can I? That would be cool." Dennis sat cross-legged in front of the walker with the box across his knees.

"The right lever controls the rudder and the left lets the sails in and out, both the main and the jib. Some of the fancier models have separate controls for each sail, but not this one."

Dennis experimented with each stick in turn. He seemed to be noting the effect on the craft. But he never achieved the speed Alex had. As he steered around the second marker, the sloop turned into the wind and came to a stop. The sails flapped helplessly. Dennis pushed and pulled the joysticks but nothing happened.

"Not aggressive enough on your tack," Alex said. "Now, as the sailors say, you're 'caught in the irons.' To get out, reverse your rudder, let out the sail, and wait."

Dennis did as directed, and the little craft drifted slowly backward and began to turn.

"Now, straighten the rudder and pull in the sails." The sloop caught wind and shot forward on a new heading.

"Major cool," said Dennis.

"No boat can sail directly into the wind," Alex advised. "The best can make about fifteen degrees off-wind, most not even that. See the little streamer attached to the top of the mast. It's called a tell-tail. It shows you which way the breeze is blowing at the sailboat. Sometimes the wind direction there is very different than here on the shore. You'll need to tack several times to reach the next marker. When you're ready to come about, back off the wind a little bit to gain speed, then quickly swing the rudder hard over."

The sun had slanted toward the horizon when Alex again looked up. *Where has the day gone?*

For hours he'd directed, taught, encouraged, and praised the student sitting cross-legged at his feet. It felt good. He admired the boy's concentration, his elation when things went well, and the short-lived despair when they didn't. Dennis had a natural talent, and Alex could tell he was a quick study.

"Getting late, son, you better head for home. Your family must be wondering where you are."

"Nah, Mom works two jobs and doesn't get home till late."

"And your dad?"

"He left when I was three. Haven't seen him since," Dennis said as he handed back the controller. "Say, could we do this again tomorrow?"

"I usually only come on Wednesdays. But... sure, why not. I bet by next week you could be a pretty good sailor. I have an old RC Laser at home. It doesn't have a jib, but it's still pretty fast. You can try it tomorrow. With two boats in the water, I'll show you how to use right-of-way to your advantage and how to steal the wind from your opponent's sails so he can't pass."

"That's awesome, man."

Together, they loaded the sloop and carrier into the old Buick.

"See you tomorrow, old man," Dennis called back as he headed through the trees toward the park exit.

Alex realized, as he turned the key and the Roadmaster's big V8 roared to life, he didn't mind being called "old man" half so much, and for the first time in a while, he didn't feel so alone.

# Gloria

Gloria Gilmore's tennis shoe was untied. She stopped at a nearby bench and, while re-tying, paused to read the inscribed commemorative brass plaque attached to the backrest.

"Dedicated to the memory of William DeHearst 1963-2007, Loving father and husband."

*The city's program of individual donations to the park seems to be working. Five new benches and several picnic tables have been added in the last year.*

She pulled the lace and retied the other shoe.

*I wonder who William DeHearst was. Only forty-four.* She paused and let out a sigh. *So young...*

She adjusted her ear-buds, turned up the volume on her iPod to block out the park noises, and returned the headband that had slipped down her forehead to its correct position. Her short, curly red hair streaked with gray was soaked from the exertion of her brisk midday jog, and she needed the band to keep sweat from dripping into her eyes.

*A couple more laps and I'll be done for today,* she thought as she returned to the asphalt path that circled the lake.

Gloria had been a runner as long as she could remember, and that was a very long time.

\*   \*   \*

Her father had started her running when she was eight years old. He always called her his 'little gazelle', because of her tall, skinny frame, and natural speed.

"I've bred a long-distance runner," he bragged to his friends. "She'll be a champion track star someday." He always smiled when he said it. His own promising Olympic career had been cut short by the war, the big one, WWII, where a bit of shrapnel in the leg had ended his hopes for a medal. She always suspected he saw in her the chance to reach that lofty goal where he had not.

Growing up on the family farm in Iowa, she and her father ran three miles each morning while her mother fixed breakfast. They repeated the routine each evening. She was ten the first time she beat her dad back to the barn.

"You'll be an Olympic champion," her dad declared when he caught his breath and could finally speak. "And you'll make us all proud."

Through high school, she entered and won all the local races, even against the boys. At a time when girls didn't excel in sports, she did. She earned a scholarship to Stanford, the first in her family to be college-bound.

*College, that's when everything changed.*

\*   \*   \*

Gloria chose a business major with a minor in athletics to keep her scholarship. "You need an education in business to fall back on," her mother insisted. "Just in case." Mom never explained what she meant by 'just in case'.

Fall was cross-country season, and Gloria practiced every day with the track team. It was the first time she'd faced stiff competition. Her local Iowa high school intramural track conference hadn't produced many female competitors. Stanford had several excellent women runners, real Olympic-caliber athletes. Gloria had been hard-pressed to keep up with the junior and senior track stars, but she'd done her best, and the coaches had been encouraging.

*       *       *

The next year, she met Norman.

She was walking across the old union between classes when she noticed a crowd near the Stanford Daily. As she got closer, Gloria realized they were chanting anti-war slogans. In the center of the group, holding a bullhorn, she saw a cute guy with unkempt, curly, deep-brown hair and black-rimmed glasses that framed intense dark gray eyes as he urged and encouraged the crowd.

After the protest was dispersed by campus police, Gloria followed the leader to the cafeteria. He took a booth at the rear of the room and was joined by two other students. She approached timidly.

When he looked up, she felt her knees weaken, but managed to stammer, "I saw you at the rally. You were wonderful."

The guy sitting next to him poked him in the ribs and said, "Whoa, Normie, I think we've got us a convert."

"Casey, let her sit down."

The young man in question quickly jumped up and, with a bow and flourish of his arm said, "Please, milady, have a seat."

She slid into the booth, and Casey moved to the opposite side.

"So, you liked what I had to say?" the leader asked.

"Very much," she replied. Actually, she couldn't remember any of his speech, but she was sure it must have been good.

"Well," he continued, "we have to make our government see the light, and protests like today are only the start."

"Uh, oh," said Casey. "Here it comes, the 'I have to speak out, it's in my blood' speech. How many times have we heard that one? All about how his dad is big in city politics. Would have been mayor, 'cept the election was rigged."

"Maybe we should introduce ourselves," the cute one interrupted. "The quiet guy over there is Brian. Wave to the lady, Brian."

Brian raised his hand and wiggled his fingers. She returned the gesture. He smiled.

"The loudmouth is Casey, and I'm Norman. You are?"

"Gloria, Gloria Wilson."

"Well, Gloria Wilson, glad to meet you."

Brian mumbled that he had a class. Casey let him out, and with a nod to the others, Brian left.

Before Casey could sit again, Norman looked at him and said, "Don't you have somewhere you need to be?"

"Don't think so... Oh! Guess I do. Thanks for reminding me. Nice to meet you, Gloria. Hope to see you again."

For the next two hours, she sat mesmerized while Norman expounded on politics, a subject she'd never given much thought.

"So, you registered for next month's election?" he asked.

"Yes, it'll be my first time voting. My dad says it's easy. He just checks the party box at the top of the ballot. Says it saves looking up all those candidates."

"What?" Norman looked shocked. "Girl, I can see you really need my help."

\*   \*   \*

Under Norman's guidance, Gloria learned to save the whales, avoid dolphin-contaminated tuna, and hug a tree. But, the most important cause was protesting the Vietnam War. She sat enthralled while he spoke at rallies, a disciple at the foot of the master. Afterward, they made love in the backseat of his Camaro.

Her family wasn't pleased with her new-found philosophy, or boyfriend. When she returned home for the Christmas holidays, she recruited several former high school friends to join her in a protest march to city hall. Her parents were shocked. Her friends just thought it was a great prank, and most of the townspeople didn't care.

"Dear, forget about this Vietnam protest thing and concentrate on your education," her mother said. "I'm worried that you're being led astray by your liberal college friends. And your dad is very angry. After all, he was wounded defending the freedoms we enjoy. We need to support our boys fighting over there, and Walter Cronkite says these protests are hurting troop morale."

"I support our soldiers," Gloria insisted holding up her left arm. "See, I have my bracelet with the name of an MIA engraved on it. I want our troops to come home. It's the government Norman and I don't trust."

Gloria and her father still ran three miles each day but rarely spoke. She'd noticed her dad slowing down and breathing heavily, even after a relatively easy workout.

\*　　\*　　\*

On her return to Stanford, she and Norman moved off-campus into an apartment. He continued to direct the local protest movement. She kept house in addition to continuing her classes, but her interests had changed to match his.

To pay their bills, she took a job as waitresses at the local diner from six to ten p.m. Norman's evenings were spent at rally planning meetings with Brian and Casey.

His weekends were filled with protest marches and sit-ins, hers with studying. Her grades slipped and her scholarship was in jeopardy.

Through it all, she'd continued to run each day, but found being the girlfriend of an activist and sole support of same exhausting. Their lovemaking waned. They squabbled over money.

"We've got the biggest protest yet planned for Friday," Norman declared as she returned home from the diner one evening. "You gotta come." He was practically jumping with excitement.

Gloria was too tired to share his enthusiasm. "You know I'm working all weekend. The rent's due again. You'll have to stop the war without me this time."

"But, babe, it'll be bitchin'. We're marching on the University Medical Center. The director fired some people, 'cause they protested. We got *beaucoup* groups joining us, including the Black Alliance and Campus Liberation Front. As Doctor King said when he spoke here last year, 'The time is now.' We're gonna face the establishment head-on and make them back down."

"You go, and when you get back, tell me all about it. Right now, I'm going to bed."

*   *   *

When Gloria returned from work, the story was all over the radio and newspapers. Two-hundred marchers had descended on the hospital director's office. He wasn't there. Norman and about sixty others then decided to stage an overnight sit-in, and occupy the administration offices, blocking entry to the surgical clinic and blood bank.

Gloria hurried to campus and tried to get near the building, but the area had been surrounded and cordoned off by the Palo Alto Police.

The next two days, she stayed glued to the news broadcasts on the radio or their small black-and-white TV. Occasionally, she caught a glimpse of Norman in negotiations with the authorities. When talks stalled after thirty hours, Police Chief Anderson declared the sit-in an 'unlawful assembly' and prepared to clear the area.

When Gloria heard sirens, she put on her cross-country shoes and ran to the campus. A large crowd had gathered.

Reinforcements from the county sheriff's office arrived and surrounded the building. Gloria and other bystanders were told to leave or be arrested. But not before she watched officers charge the building and break in the medical center's north door.

"No!" Gloria screamed. She was shocked that the sit-in had turned violent and was terrified that Norman would be arrested, injured, or worse.

Newspapers later reported that the demonstrators inside had fought back, throwing office equipment, including typewriters and a steno machine, at the police. One officer had been knocked unconscious and several others had been injured. The cops had regrouped and charged again. This time, they'd been driven back by high-pressure streams from the building's fire hoses.

Safely back in their apartment, Gloria waited nervously. Finally, around ten o'clock, she heard a noise at the door. Norman stood there, bruised and dirty, with what looked like blood on his sweatshirt.

"Got to lay low for a while, babe," he said. Then he added, pointing to the stain on his shirt, "It's not mine. A guy got clubbed right next to me. When the cops came through the north door, we ducked out the east. A cop hit Brian, and he went down, but a bunch of us made it. We outnumbered the guards covering the east door and bowled right through 'em. I kept running as fast as I could, then hid out till dark. Don't know what happened to Casey. Didn't see if he made it."

"What about Brian?" Gloria had asked.

Norman just shrugged, and then quickly stuffed clothes into a duffel bag. "Just play dumb and tell the cops you haven't seen me."

At the door, he kissed her.

She watched from the porch as the Camaro roared to life, pulled out of the carport, and disappeared into the night.

*     *     *

The next day she found Brian in the hospital and went to see him. He'd suffered a severe concussion, a broken arm, and cracked ribs. He was sleeping when she entered his room. For several hours, she sat by his bedside and held his hand.

The following day, he was awake but groggy when she visited. The doctor suggested she talk to him. She described all the events that had taken place.

"But I don't remember anything," he said. "Last thing I recall was hearing the cop's bullhorn telling us to leave. Then I woke up here. Where is everyone?"

"Norman left town. I don't know about Casey, but since he's not in jail or here, I assume he escaped too."

Brian was discharged four days later, promptly arrested, charged with a misdemeanor, and released on his own recognizance with a warning that a hearing date for his case would be set soon. Gloria met him outside the police station.

"I've been tossed out of the dorm and have nowhere to stay," he moaned. "My parents haven't answered any of my calls."

"Well, there's a sofa in my apartment you can use if you don't find something better," she offered.

But Brian hadn't found anything better and showed up at the door later that afternoon with his suitcase in his good hand.

His other arm was in a cast, his ribs were taped, and he still experienced occasional dizzy spells. Gloria insisted it would be better if he took the bed. She offered to sleep on the couch. He reluctantly agreed.

After some time, they settled into a routine, just like brother and sister.

Since Norman had left his clothes all over the house for her to pick up, Gloria was surprised that Brian was neat, did his own laundry, knocked before entering a room, and made the bed each morning. He even got up early and started the coffee.

After he healed enough, he switched to the couch, giving her back her bedroom.

Where they had barely spoken before, now, thrown together, she was surprised to learn Brian was a serious pre-med student who wanted to start his own general practice when he finished school. With Brian, life was much quieter and more comfortable.

For three months, they heard nothing from Norman. Then, late one evening, she answered the doorbell. There he stood. He'd grown a beard. It was redder than his dark hair, but just as curly.

"Hi, babe. Miss me?" he asked before pulling her into an embrace and long, passionate kiss. He swept her into his arms and carried her to the bedroom, where they caught up on what they'd missed during his absence.

Brian found other accommodations.

*   *   *

Life with Norman was always exciting. The apartment again became the meeting place for planning rallies and campus protests. Gloria came home from working at the diner to find her home full of people discussing politics over empty pizza boxes and spent beer cans. Casey, who had been hiding at his aunt's house in Fresno, returned and was as vocal as ever. But Brian stayed away.

Carrying out the trash one evening, she realized some of the luster of her life with Norman had worn off. Quirks she hadn't noticed before, now annoyed her. Like his throwing his wet towel on the bathroom floor after showering, leaving it for her to hang up. When she complained, Norman said he had too many other more important things on his mind, but he'd try to remember. He never did.

Several weeks later, she saw Brian crossing the campus and ran to meet him.

"Haven't seen you around lately. You all right?" she inquired.

"Sure, I'm fine. In addition to my classes, I volunteer at the hospital now. It's giving me some on-the-job training. We really messed the place up with the sit-in. A hundred-thousand dollars in damages. It took weeks to get the place back to normal. We need to think about who our protests really hurt. I told Norman I'm not coming back."

*     *     *

Then, in late March when she returned to their apartment, Norman's beat up Camaro was gone from the carport. The apartment was quiet and empty. Norman's belongings were gone. Wadded up in the trash, she found his draft induction notice.

A few days later, she discovered her savings account had been cleaned out, and her credit card statement showed she had paid for gas for the Camaro all the way to the Canadian border.

She remembered he'd warned, "They'll never draft me. I'll be out of the country before those establishment pigs can catch up."

He'd made good his escape, which, she now realized, didn't include her.

She cancelled the credit card.

Her folks wired her enough money to pay the rent. She suspected they were secretly pleased that Norman was gone.

"We knew that boy wasn't good for you," her mother confided over the phone. "Now, maybe you'll concentrate on your studies and your scholarship. Forget about all this protest nonsense."

"Yes, Mother," she answered. "I'll see you at the end of June. And this is only a loan. I promise I'll pay you back."

"That's all right, dear. You know your father and I only want the best for our little gazelle."

The next day in the cafeteria, Brian approached her table.

"Gloria, are you all right?" His voice sounded concerned. "Casey told me Norman split."

"Yes, he's gone," she confided.

"Well, if you need a friend, I'm here."

"Thanks. I'll remember that."

\*     \*     \*

As the end of spring quarter approached, Gloria found it harder and harder to keep up at track practice. She thought she'd caught the flu. But the nausea didn't go away. At the clinic, they confirmed she was pregnant.

"Pregnant? I can't be!" she exclaimed.

"Rabbits don't lie," the doctor insisted. "You're about ten weeks along."

All the way home and into the night, she cried.

*What am I going to do? I can't tell my parents. They'd be so hurt, and they've done so much for me already. No, I have to solve this on my own.*

By morning, she'd decided an abortion was the only logical answer. But she lacked the funds to pay for one.

"Brian works at the hospital. Maybe he can find someone to help," she told herself in the mirror.

She met Brian for lunch in the cafeteria. There, between sobs, she told him the whole story and her decision.

Brian was silent for a minute, and then said, "There is another option, you know. You could marry me."

"But..." she began.

"No! Listen," he interrupted. "I've loved you ever since that first day we met. But you were Norman's girl, and I wasn't going to interfere."

"But, I don't think I love you, Brian, at least not that way."

"I know, but I hope in time you will. Give me a chance to convince you. It's much better than an abortion."

"You'd do that for me?"

"In a heartbeat," he answered. "I think a Vegas wedding is in order, don't you?"

\*     \*     \*

They married the following weekend with Casey as best man. When her parents found out, they were incensed and refused to speak to her. But after Heather Marguerite Gilmore was born, they came around. Their grandchild made all the difference.

It took Brian an extra year to finish his internship. Gloria continued to work nights at the diner. Brian spent his days at the hospital. They each took charge of Heather when the other was working, but it left little time for the two adults to be alone.

*Brian takes great care of Heather. He loves her like his own. He's such a great dad. I wish she were his child,* Gloria thought while watching them play together.

Finally, following Brian's graduation, the family moved to Southern California to be near his parents and open his practice.

When Heather started school, Gloria worked as Brian's receptionist in the office. She still ran in local 10K events occasionally but the dream of Olympic gold was far behind her.

And Gloria grew to love Brian. Oh, not with the white-hot, passionate lust she'd felt for Norman. But deep warmth permeated her soul whenever she thought of him. She finally confessed her love one day as they shared lunch.

Brian looked startled, then he smiled and took her hand. "For the first couple of years, I was afraid if Norman came back, you'd immediately leave me to be with him."

"I don't think I'd have been that stupid. Norman's not the marrying or fatherly type," Gloria confessed. "And believe me, when we married, it was for keeps. You're the one I want to spend the rest of my life with."

The years passed, and life was good.

\*     \*     \*

"Talked to Casey the other day," Brian announced at breakfast one day. "He told me Norman returned to the states in the mid-nineties, moved to San Francisco to fight for a new cause. Gay rights. He and his partner, Shaun, organized rallies and marches just like in the old days. Casey located them about two years ago. I thought you'd like to know."

"I haven't thought about Norman for a long time," she admitted.

"Casey called to tell us Norman's partner died last year of AIDS. Norman's in the last stages. He's been moved to a nursing facility in Daily City and he asked for you. Casey thinks it would be good if you went see him." Brian paused. "I think so too. You have unfinished business."

"But I can't..." she began.

"I've already made reservations. You fly out Friday morning. I can take care of myself."

*   *   *

Entering Norman's room, she saw a stranger lying in the bed. The dark curly hair was gone, replaced by a bald head. The emaciated body bore little resemblance to the man she remembered. A thin arm with red and purple welts lay on top of the blanket; a plastic tube extended to the IV bag hanging nearby.

"Norman?" she asked.

His turned his eyes toward her and they widened in recognition.

"Hi, babe," he muttered in a whispered voice. "Been a long time, hasn't it?"

"It sure has," she replied.

"Sorry I ran out on you. Didn't know what else to do. Been thinking a lot about you lately. My leaving must have hurt. I'm so sorry." He paused. "You know," he began again, but had to stop as several dry, rasping, coughs racked his body. "I've been dissatisfied my whole life, always looking to change the world. Now, I realize, it's the world that changed me. I feel like I never accomplished anything important. What a waste."

Gloria sighed. "I wouldn't say that. I see your image in our daughter."

"We have a daughter?"

"Yes, her name is Heather. She's a lawyer with the Public Defender's Office in Dallas. Where she got that idea, I don't know. She must have picked up your protest gene, though. Oh, she's not as wild, but in a small way, very like you.

"When she was a junior in high school, she discovered the cafeteria was adding surplus cottage cheese to the hamburger meat. She got her friends to protest, even making posters saying, 'No More Gray Burgers.' The school board changed the policy. Brian and I were so proud."

"Brian? Quiet, Brian?"

"My husband, yes. We could never have any more children of our own. He says you gave him the two greatest gifts he ever received."

He nodded with the sheen of unshed tears in his eyes.

"Time for your medication," the nurse said, entering the room. Norman took the pills she handed him with the paper cup of water.

After the nurse left, he said, "Those meds don't do shit. Would you look in the top drawer? There's some cigarette paper and, behind the cabinet, you'll find my stash."

She followed his directions, rolled the weed into the wrapper, and twisted the ends before handing it to him. He lit up and inhaled deeply.

"I remember when we did this stuff for fun. Now it's the only thing that helps the pain and nausea. The staff knows I have it. They just pretend it's not here." Norman leaned back and closed his eyes. "So, she takes after her old man, huh? Will you stay with me till the drugs take effect and I fall asleep?"

Gloria held his hand. His head drooped and his breathing slowed. She removed the remaining stub from his lips and crushed out the end before throwing it away.

"Goodbye," she whispered.

\* \* \*

Gloria finished her last lap of the park and jogged to her waiting car.

Looking at her watch, she thought, *Almost four-o'clock, Brian will leave the office in half an hour. I'd better get home.*

She looked at the nearby bench again.

*A memorial for Norman? After all, without him, I never would have found my true love, nor had a wonderful daughter like Heather. Yes, a bench with a brass plaque. Brian will agree.*

# Alice

"Would you two like to hear a joke?" Alice inquired.

The power walkers paused in their noontime ritual, three laps around Lakeview Park, and turned to see who had spoken. Before them stood a smiling grandmotherly type, her white hair cut short and curled to frame her plump face. Light blue eyes were complimented by her pale yellow blouse, white slacks, and pastel blue overshirt. They'd seen her before during their daily noon walks and listened to her joke already. But to be polite...

"Sure, we'd love to hear it," one replied.

Happy to have a receptive audience, she shifted into her best imitation of a New England accent and began.

"Were you in the boat when the boat tipped over?" She paused for the punch line. "No, kind sir, I was in the water."

The men laughed, thanked her, and continued on their walk.

*Such nice young men*, she thought as she watched them follow the path until they disappeared from view behind a row of eucalyptus. She gazed a moment at her surroundings. The fall sun felt warm but not hot, the air fresh, the sky blue and cloudless.

*This is such a lovely park; I wish I'd come here earlier.*

*Earlier than what?* her mind asked.

*I don't know,* she replied, a little irritated at the thought. *Just earlier.*

She continued on the asphalt path that rounded the lake until she came to the old wooden bridge connecting the island and the larger, lower lake. Three mallards circled overhead and glided in formation for a feet-extended perfect landing at the water's edge.

*Yes, what a beautiful day,* Alice thought to herself. She'd have said it out loud if there had been anyone nearby.

Ahead, a man approached. He walked swiftly and seemed to be talking constantly to himself. As he got closer, she could hear part of his conversation.

"Yes, Jeff, we need to be on top of this one. Call Anderson and set up a conference... No, no need for me to be there. I'm sure you can handle it."

"Would you like to hear a joke?" Alice asked.

"Can't you see I'm on the phone?" the man retorted and brushed past. She watched as he marched away, the sound of his voice fading in the distance.

*How rude!* She had, of course, noticed the large black hearing aid he was wearing. *He must be nearly deaf.* Her own units were small, flesh-colored, and hidden mostly inside her ears.

"I'll give him the benefit of the doubt," she said. "He just didn't hear me."

*After all, who wouldn't like a good joke?*

Still, his abruptness had taken some of the joy from her outing. She resolved to try another person.

A hundred yards up the path, a young woman sat on a park bench, a stroller at her side. At the edge of the lake, a child tossed pieces of bread to a growing group of assorted ducks, geese, and pigeons. Several seagulls hovered overhead, waiting to steal from the flocks below.

"Joey, don't get too close to the water," the mother warned as Alice approached.

*Good, she speaks English*, Alice thought. One time she had tried to tell her joke to another woman, only to find that she understood no English, and Alice knew no other language.

*How long ago was that?* Alice couldn't remember.

"Would you like to hear a joke?"

"Joey, I told you, not that close. You don't want me to have to come over there."

Little Joey, with a glance his mother's way, ripped another piece of bread from the slice he carried, purposely stepped toward the lake edge, and overhanded the morsel toward a far duck.

"Joey Carson, get over here this minute!" Mother was on her feet and headed toward the boy. She grasped his arm above the elbow and started dragging him away from the lakefront.

"Gee, Mom," he complained, "I still got some bread left."

"You can use it tomorrow. Your father will be home soon. You and your little sister both need baths before dinner."

Alice watched as the young woman pushed the infant-filled stroller and pulled the reluctant Joey up the path toward the parking lot.

*Guess she didn't hear me either. Doesn't anyone want to listen to my joke? Well, a young mother like that is probably too busy to listen to an old woman like me.*

Alice sat on the vacated bench. She seemed to remember when she had small children, but much as she tried, the memories were indistinct. Only little snippets of long ago. *There was a son, Greg, I think, and a daughter.* She sat on the bench for what seemed a long time.

Two men walked quickly up the path toward her. As they passed she tried again.

"Would you two like to hear a joke?"

They'd seen her already during their previous lap around the lake, and had listened to her joke before. But to be polite...

"Sure, we'd love to hear it," one replied.

She put on her best New England accent and remembered to pause before the punchline.

The men laughed, thanked her, and continued their walk.

As they disappeared behind a grove of eucalyptus, it seemed all too familiar.

*Did I see those men earlier?*

The sun slipped behind a cloud causing her to look up. A chill breeze began to blow from across the lake. She pulled her shirt closer around her.

*I'd better get home,* she thought. *Home, HOME? Where is home?* She couldn't remember. Everything outside the park was a mystery. She was lost.

Panic filled her. The park, so beautiful just moments before, was now menacing. Trees that had sheltered now pressed in around her. Alice clung to the arm of the bench like a sailor on a stormy sea and searched for something familiar, anything.

"Alice, Alice," a distant voice called her name. *Yes, that's my name... Alice.*

A nice older man in blue jeans and work shirt came quickly up the path and stopped in front of the bench where she sat.

"Hi, Alice, my name's Carlos. Remember? I'm the head groundskeeper here. The walkers said you were down by the lake again. I called the nursing home and they're sending someone for you. They'll meet us at the entrance like they always do. Your son, Greg, and his family have been looking for you for several hours."

He held out his strong, calloused hand. She placed hers in his. Together, they walked toward the main parking lot.

*Such a nice man*, she thought.

"Would you like to hear a joke?"

# Carl

Eleven-thirty exactly. Carl pulled the Nissan pickup into the park entry road. Carl was always prompt, especially when he was going to meet Sylvia. It was the highlight of his day.

He passed the crowded east lot and followed the narrow one-lane road lined with its cut log border to the less-used north lot. Here he could always find an open stall near where she parked in the shade of the towering eucalyptus that ringed the parking area. He locked the door and walked a few feet to the bench at the edge of the walking path, sat, and waited. Fifteen minutes passed.

*She must be running behind today*, he thought.

Finally, he saw her head, followed by the rest of her body, rise into view where the path crested the slight hill at the far side of the upper lake. It reminded him of the first time he'd seen her.

\*   \*   \*

He'd only been discharged from the service for two months and just taken the job at the auto parts store. In high school, he'd worked the night shift at the Richfield station. He'd had few friends and didn't want more.

His was one of the few remaining stations to provide a full-service lane. By the time the military finished with him, everything was self-serve with no need for more than one attendant to sit in a locked booth, reset pumps, and take money. He didn't like the new system.

Besides, the California Air National Guard, in true military wisdom and aware of his previous experience, had assigned him to the motor pool. Not working on vehicles, but in procurement; ordering, expediting, shipping, and generally making sure the right parts got to the right places at the right time to keep the military machine running. Never much for paperwork, he was now inundated with forms, and in time became efficient. He rode out the First Gulf War from a desk at the 129th Air Rescue and Resupply Group based at Moffett Field, California.

PepBoys was more of the same. He didn't work the front counter, didn't have to face customers in person. Rather, he manned the phones, ordered parts, maintained stock, and handled the commercial accounts and car dealerships.

And he was still there.

He'd taken to walking in the park at lunch each day just to get out of the building. And one day he noticed her.

She'd been a runner then, wearing track shorts and a tank top. At first sight, her beauty had, as they say, taken his breath away. She was tall, at least half-a-foot taller than his five-foot-seven. Distance-runner thin with long legs and long blonde hair hanging nearly to her waist and tied in a ponytail that swung from side to side with each stride.

That first day when she ran past, he had to look away as she approached so she wouldn't notice he was staring. Once she went by, his gaze followed her until she disappeared beyond the trees at the far end of the lower lake.

Carl soon learned her schedule and adjusted his. Each workday, he jogged counter-clockwise around the lake knowing she always ran clockwise. This meant they passed often on the path. Even after several weeks, he hadn't found the courage to speak. Then an opportunity presented itself.

Noting her loose laces as they passed one day, he called, "Careful, your shoe's untied."

"Thank you," she replied in a voice breathy from exertion. He stopped, placing his hands on his knees as if to catch his own breath. It was an excuse to watch as she retied the one shoe and then tightened the laces on the other at a nearby bench before sprinting off.

Several more weeks went by. Their encounters now included a nod or wave of acknowledgement in passing, but nothing more. Carl tried unsuccessfully to think of some way to bridge this impasse.

Finally, the woman herself solved the problem. He'd just parked when she appeared at his window.

"Say, if we're going to meet like this every day, maybe we should introduce ourselves. I'm Sylvia," she said, extending her hand.

For a second, he was stunned. *She spoke to me.* Finally he managed a weak, "Hello, S-S-Sylvia. My name is Carl. It's nice to meet you."

That day, he changed direction and ran with her. She was in better condition, and he was soon laboring to keep up. After two quick laps she slowed to a cool-down walk.

It was perfect; Carl was in heaven until he noticed the wedding ring on her left hand.

*Carl, you fool. Even if she weren't married, she'd never be interested in someone like you.*

But he continued to run with her. He couldn't stay away.

\*   \*   \*

"Hey, earth to Carl," Sylvia's familiar voice broke into his thoughts. "Are we walking today? Or what?"

The woman who stood before Carl now was fifteen years older, a little heavier, and white streaks accented the blonde, shoulder-length hair. But he still thought she was beautiful.

Today, Sylvia wore gray sweatpants and a white tee-shirt. She smiled down at him. He smiled back.

"Sure, let's go," he said, quickly getting to his feet and tying the sleeves of his sweatshirt around his waist.

Now they walked. Running hadn't survived the first year, and even jogging had ceased after the birth of Sylvia's second child, Carrie. Besides, it was much easier to talk at the slower pace. And talk they did. Well, mostly he listened.

Conversation usually centered on the weather, her family, and current events. Still, that first year he learned much about her husband, David, five-year-old son, Ron, her job, and David's career. When asked, Carl told a little of his life and working at the parts house. He knew he was boring. But he loved to listen to her voice.

They had never touched. Well there was that one time.

\*   \*   \*

Sylvia had been seven-and-a-half months pregnant with her second child and showing. She was sitting on the bench near the north lot when he arrived.

"Are you up to this today?" Carl asked, noting dark circles beneath her eyes.

"I think so," she replied. "I've been having some pains, false labor the doctor thinks. This has been a much tougher pregnancy than Ron's. I'll be glad when it's over."

About halfway around the lake, she stopped suddenly, bent over, and put her hands to her knees. "I think my water just broke," she announced. "I need to get to the hospital. Help me, Carl."

He took her left hand and wrapped his arm around her back to lift and steady her. Together they made their way to her car. Carefully placing Sylvia in the passenger seat and taking the keys, he started the engine and headed for Memorial Hospital, about fifteen minutes away.

"It's too soon," she kept murmuring between contractions that were becoming more regular and, as he could see, stronger. Carl pressed the accelerator a little harder trying to shorten the trip.

At the Emergency entrance, a nurse helped Sylvia into a wheelchair.

"Please call David at work and tell him," she said, handing Carl a slip of paper with a number written on it. He headed for the pay phones in the lobby.

*I've never talked to David, or any of Sylvia's family or friends*, Carl thought. *Does he know about me? Has she told him?* Carl fumbled in his pocket for change. *No dimes, but here's a quarter. That'll do.* Hearing the tone, he dialed the number and, when directed, inserted the quarter into the phone slot.

"David Marshal Insurance, David speaking," a smooth baritone voice answered.

"Your wife, Sylvia, has gone into labor and is at Memorial Hospital."

Carl heard a moment's silence, then, "She's not due yet. Who is this?"

Carl was at a loss. *Does he know me? Would he recognize the name?* He glanced at the sign on the doorway across from the phone and answered in his most professional voice. "This is the Tedford Medical Group; your wife has requested we call you."

"Tell her I'm on my way." The line went dead.

Carl took a taxi back to the park. But he returned to the hospital that night to look through the nursery glass at a small newborn wrapped in a pink blanket. A girl. He'd always felt close to Carrie, even though they'd never met.

\*      \*      \*

"Have you heard anything I've said?" Sylvia looked cross.

Carl blinked back to the present. "Oh, I'm sorry. What was that?"

"I was talking about the holidays. Thanksgiving is next week with Christmas and New Year's Eve not far behind. You're always welcome at our house. Although I don't know why I keep asking; you never come. We're having turkey, and Ron will be on break from freshman year at college. I'm anxious to spend some time with him."

"Naw. I wouldn't want to be in the way," Carl said. "Besides, I have other plans."

"I've heard that one before. You say it every year," she responded. "Anyway, it's not just family. My friend,

Joyce, will be there. You have so much in common. She isn't married either. I've been trying to get the two of you together for years."

"Another reason to decline." He grinned. "I'm not the marrying kind."

"Well, if you change your mind, there'll be food, and good company," she said, turning off the path toward the parking area and her car. As she unlocked and opened the driver-side door, she added, "Besides, our walks may come to an end soon."

Carl's breath caught in his throat and his stomach knotted. "What?"

"David's business hasn't done very well recently. What with the economy and all, he thinks we ought to move out-of-state. It's too expensive here. We'll try to hold off until June. I don't want Carrie to have to leave all her friends just before mid-high graduation. It's a very important time for a girl. If we can make it till then, we'll move during summer vacation so Carrie can enroll in a different high school."

Carl stood unmoving and watched as she drove away.

\* \* \*

That night, alone in his large, sparsely-furnished apartment, Carl couldn't concentrate. He burned the canned tomato soup but broke enough saltine crackers into the bowl to somewhat hide the charred flavor. He ate it anyway.

"She might leave," he kept repeating, as if saying the words aloud could change the reality.

His secret hope that she might someday divorce David and be free to be with him finally died. Now, sitting in front of the TV, dirty bowl and spoon on the coffee table, he realized she'd never, could never, leave her husband. And even if she did, she'd never be his.

"She'll move away and leave me," he said to the TV.

*   *   *

As predicted, Carl didn't make it to Sylvia's for Thanksgiving. He ate a Swanson turkey dinner at home while watching the Packer's game. The following day at the park, Sylvia complained, "You missed a great meal. David said it was one of my best. Ron and Carrie both were disappointed when you weren't there."

"They know about me?"

"They know you're my friend and that we walk around the lake each day. I've never kept you a secret. Although, you're kind of a mystery man to the children, like Santa Claus or the Tooth Fairy." She chuckled.

"Bet you all have a good laugh about the strange guy at the park." Carl's anger flared at her assumed betrayal.

"No," Sylvia said. "It's not like that. They've heard so much about you all their lives and have never seen you, that's all."

Carl was still smarting after the walk and decided to not go to the park the following Monday. *That'll show her.*

After his one-day protest, he was right on time Tuesday. But Sylvia didn't come. Carl waited several hours. She wasn't there the following day, or the next. Carl began to worry that something serious had happened. That she wasn't ever coming back.

*Have they moved already?*

Finally, after a week, he worked up the courage to phone her home.

"Hello," answered a soft, young female voice.

"Is Sylvia there?"

"No. Can I take a message? She should be back later on."

He took a deep breath. "Just tell her Carl called."

"Carl, it's you!" the voice exclaimed. "This is Carrie. Mom's at Memorial Hospital. Ron was in a car accident. She said to let you know if you called. He's hurt pretty bad, but the doctors say he's gonna make it."

*   *   *

When Carl found Ron's room, Sylvia wasn't there. A young man attached by tubes and cables to monitoring devices occupied one of the beds. He opened an eye as Carl entered.

"Hello Ron, my name's Carl. I heard you were in an accident. Came over to see how you're doing. Bet you're surprised to meet me."

A slight smile crossed the boy's face. He nodded stiffly and motioned for Carl to sit next to the bed. Carl noted the feeding tube down Ron's throat.

"Since you can't talk, I'll have to do it for both of us. I've heard about you all your life. Your mother loves you very much."

Carl repeated stories he'd heard on those many laps around the lake. About Ron's triumphs in sports, his good grades, the Christmas when he was eight and got his first two-wheeled bike, both the good times and the not-so-good.

As he spoke, Carl realized he knew more about Sylvia's family than he did about his friends and co-workers at the store.

*I've lived my life through Sylvia and her family,* he thought. *Maybe it's time I started living my own.*

After half an hour, Carl announced, "I'll come to see you again, Ron."

*     *     *

Sylvia spent her free time with Ron at the hospital and no longer joined Carl at the park. Carl's walks were solitary. After several days alone, he decided one afternoon to see Ron again. The boy was awake and sitting up in bed when Carl entered.

"Carl, you do exist," the boy exclaimed. "With all the meds I was on, I thought I might have imagined you. How come you only show up when no one else is around?"

"I don't like crowds," Carl admitted, pulling the guest chair closer to the bed. "You certainly look better. I see all the tubes have been removed."

"The doctors say I can be home for Christmas. It won't be like normal, though. Dad's already in Seattle setting up the new business, and as soon as the house sells, Ma will quit her job and she and Carrie will head there, too. When I'm better, I'll go back to college. Got a scholarship to maintain, ya know."

"So your family is actually moving." *Better get used to it, Carl.*

"Yeah, my accident was kinda the last straw. They say it's pretty nice up there, if you don't mind all the rain." He laughed, then paused. "But, I'm worried about losing my resident status when they move. We have no other family here and non-resident tuition is a lot more than my scholarship. We won't be able to afford it. Ma's been looking into a student loan. But, I don't know." His voice trailed off.

Carl sat for a minute, thinking. *Maybe I can help.*

"You know, Ron," Carl began. "In the fifteen years we've walked the park together, hearing all about you and Carrie..." Carl paused. "You and your sister have sort of become like family to me. The family I've never had. I may have a solution. There's a small spare bedroom and bath at my place. Why don't you move in with me and use my address?"

"You'd do that for me?" Ron looked amazed.

"Sure, after all, what's a friend for if he can't help out?" Carl concluded.

\* \* \*

Leaving the hospital, Carl walked with a lighter step. *Maybe, just maybe I should consider going to the Christmas party this year. After all, Ron wants me to come, and I haven't seen Carrie since she was an infant. I'll call Sylvia. She might just invite that Joyce she's been pushing at me. Could be interesting.*

# Carolina

Every other Thursday in June, July, and August, the city sponsored 'Concerts on the Green' at Lakeview Park. A stage was constructed near the picnic area and bands were invited to perform. People brought dinner, set lawn chairs and blankets on the grass, and enjoyed the entertainment.

For Carlos, it meant overtime. While he didn't much care for the extra hours, the pay was good, and since he was approaching retirement, any extra money he could put aside was appreciated. Sometimes Maria would join him, but on the evening of the first concert of the year, he was alone.

Following the event, Carlos stored the sound equipment, removed chairs from the stage, and locked everything movable in the shed before turning off the floodlights. In the morning, he'd join Tom to pick up debris left by the guests.

After eleven p.m., he finally headed for his car, his flashlight illuminating the asphalt path. It was then he heard a far-off cry. It seemed to be coming from the south end of the lake. A woman's voice. He couldn't make out the words, but she sounded desperate. He headed that direction.

At first, Carlos couldn't find the source of the voice. He panned the beam around the shore, and saw nothing. Something made him switch off the flashlight. The waning moon cast a pale sheen on the landscape, the trees on the far side making black shadows across the water.

"Help me please," the voice entreated. "She's lost and I cannot find her."

"Who's lost?" he called back. "Where are you?"

Then he saw her. She was pushing her way through tall grasses and reeds toward him. She looked in his direction, her face in the moonlight a mask of anguish and pain.

"Who are you looking for?" Carlos called across the water. He switched on the light and panned the shoreline for anyone else, then shined his light toward the woman. She was gone! Only silent, clear, rippling water remained.

Carlos's mind reeled; where she had been standing, the water had to be twenty-feet deep.

*The lake's always kept free of any growth. What's going on?*

All was silent. The lady did not reappear, even when he turned off the flashlight. Carlos drove home but didn't tell Maria what he'd seen.

The next morning, Carlos reported the incident to his supervisor, expecting not to be believed.

"I swear. You know I don't drink, but it was so strange. First she was there; then she wasn't. I didn't ever believe in ghosts, but after last night, I'm not so sure."

"Well, Carlos," Daniel replied, "I've been around since the park was dedicated back in 1968 and haven't seen anything like that. However, there was an article in the local paper a few years back about ghosts in this area. I think it was written by someone at the Historical Society. You might want to check there."

All morning, the expression on the face of the woman Carlos had encountered the night before haunted his thoughts. Preoccupied, he forgot to reset the sprinkler timer delayed for the concert, and the water came on wetting the fishermen at the north end of the lake. He hurriedly apologized and cut off the spray.

*Maybe Daniel's right. Perhaps someone can help.*

At lunchtime, Carlos headed for the County Historical Society.

\*     \*     \*

"So you've seen the ghost?" Mildred, the head historian, a thin freckle-faced lady in her late fifties, inquired. "You're not alone. There have been several reported sightings over the past hundred years, but nothing since the old Union Wells Reservoir was turned into a permanent lake and the park build around it.

"It's a very sad story," she continued. "The legend says it's the ghost of Mrs. Methven, searching for her lost child. I think there's even a picture of her in our files."

She led Carlos into a back room. Bookshelves and file cabinets lined the walls. Several large flat files occupied the center. Mildred approached one of these.

"That would be about 1901," she murmured, scanning down the line of drawers. She opened one, looked in, then closed it and opened the one below.

"Here it is," she said excitedly as she put on white gloves and removed a folder. She opened it. "It says:

'Andrew Methven and his wife, Carolina, were three years married when they arrived from Pasadena in1892. He bought a parcel of about nine acres adjacent to the Union Wells Reservoir and built a modest home, consisting of three rooms.

'Andrew was employed as a fumigator, a dangerous but highly lucrative job. Orange trees had to be tented and sprayed with lethal chemicals to maintain a good crop.

'Their daughter, Felicia, was born in 1895.'"

"Here's the picture." She held up an aged eight-by-ten sepia photo in a protective sleeve.

Carlos saw a young woman, her dark hair done up in two braids, coiled and fastened on each side of her head. She wore a high-collared white blouse, floor-length black skirt and matching jacket. Her right arm rested on the back of an ornate chair, the left hand covering the right. But it was the face, the deep-set eyes, the straight nose and serious expression, which commanded his attention.

*It's the same face as the other night. That's her.*

Below the picture was written in faded script, *Carolina Methven-1901.*

Carlos's breath caught in his throat and he felt the hair on his arms stand up as if from a sudden chill.

Mildred continued reading:

'Andrew and Carolina doted on their only daughter. He even made a playhouse for her using tule from the reservoir for the sides and palm fronds for the roof. She and school friends would often play there as it was on the waterfront path between her home and the one-room schoolhouse about four miles away.'

Mildred produced a picture of the reservoir from the file. It looked nothing like the manicured, cement-lined lake Carlos maintained. Rather, it resembled a low swamp with reeds and grasses growing in the shallows. The tall stands of eucalyptus were missing. Only a few scrub oak dotted the bank. Behind could be seen several wooden oil drilling derricks.

'During the winter of 1904, rains in the foothills caused a flash flood that overflowed the lake and inundated the Methven home. Andrew and Carolina survived by climbing orange trees. Felicia, thought to be at the playhouse, was never found. Carolina fell into a deep depression and died the following spring, some say of a broken heart. In 1909, Andrew lost his life when he accidentally inhaled too much of the poison gas used on the trees. The first appearance of the ghost was around that time.'

"I have several newspaper accounts of sightings," Mildred said. "Would you like to see those? Most often, people heard a woman crying late at night and mysterious footprints were found along the bank. After the reservoir was drained and the lake constructed in 1967, the sightings stopped. I think Mr. Peterson is the only other person still living who saw her. Till you, of course. He's at the Lakeview Care Center. He's ninety-two years old and still tells the story to any who will listen."

Mildred showed him several of the accounts. Carlos thanked her and returned to work.

*     *     *

"I'm glad you told me," Maria said at breakfast several days later. "You've been so quiet and preoccupied lately, I was beginning to worry."

"I can't get her face out of my mind. It's like... I don't know... Like she looked right at me and wants me to help her somehow. I just don't know how. Maybe I need to drop by the nursing home and see what Mr. Peterson can tell me."

*     *     *

The following week, Carlos visited the Lakeside Extended Care Center. He'd been there several times before, usually to return Alice Sullivan, a senile dementia patent, who would occasionally wander onto the park property and become lost.

"Frank Peterson is in room 121," said the young Asian nurse in a pale blue uniform as he signed in at the reception desk. "Down that hallway, turn left at the corridor. It's the second room on the right."

Carlos thanked her and headed for the room. He found Frank dozing in his wheelchair next to the bed. A plastic tube was clipped to his nose and draped over his ears to an oxygen tank strapped to the chair. When Carlos brought up the subject of the lady at the lake, Frank was more than happy to repeat his story to a new, interested audience. Carlos listened intently.

"I often worked late on the drilling rigs," Frank said in voice hardly more than a whisper and punctuated with long inhaled breaths as he tried to get more air into his lungs. "I walked past the old lake on my way home each night... Saw her several times, but could never get close... She sure seemed like a nice lady, though. I really wanted to help her... 'Course, now I'm trapped here attached to this damn air tank. Emphysema, you know. Too much time in the oil fields, too many years smoking... Doctors said I could go at any time. I think I'm about ready; don't know why God's kept me here this long."

Carlos told Frank of his meeting with the lady and what he'd learned from the historical society.

"Carolina's her name, huh? Wish I'd known it back then... I think she heard me once... You gonna try to see her after your next concert? Real nice lady, sorry she's so sad."

After Frank drifted to sleep in his chair, Carlos quietly left the room.

*       *       *

"You know, you don't need to work the concert tonight," Daniel repeated for the third time. "I can get Tom to stay late, if you'd rather go home."

"No, I have a strange feeling I need to be here tonight. I can't explain it. I know it's been affecting my work. I'll try to do better next week."

The concert featured a local rock band; the crowd was younger, more rowdy. It had not been one of Carlos's favorite evenings. He closed and locked the shed, turned out the park floodlights and listened in the dark. No sound.

*She's not going to show.*

After an hour, Carlos picked up his flashlight but didn't turn it on. Slowly he started for the car. There were no clouds and the now-full moon gave plenty of light. He had purposely parked at the south end, so he'd be forced to walk the length of the silent lake.

The voice! Now he heard it. He hurried toward the source, being careful not to trip on the darkened path. Then he saw her on the far side, standing in the shallows. But she was not alone. A man stood on the shore and beckoned her to him. She went. He took her hand, and together they disappeared into the shade of the overhanging trees.

*       *       *

The obituary read:

Frank Peterson, long-time resident of the city, died Thursday evening July sixteenth at the age of ninety-two, following a long illness. Internment is scheduled for Friday, July twenty-fourth at Cityside Memorial Park. Mr. Peterson will be buried beside his wife, Edith, who preceded him in death. He had no known surviving relatives.

*I wonder what Frank said to make her go with him,* Carlos thought. *Must have convinced her he'd help find her daughter. Bet they did.*

# Tiffany

"You like my brother? Yuck!" Zoe exclaimed as they exited sixth period math and pushed through the crush of students at the front door of Lakeview High.

"You don't have to broadcast it to the world," Tiffany whispered once they'd passed the gaggle of sophomores on the front steps. "I only told you 'cause you're my best friend." Mentally Tiffany added. *And if I'd known you were going to blab it all over the school, I wouldn't have. I've had a crush on your big brother since fifth grade.*

"Well, if you're so stuck on him, Zack's giving me a ride home today. You might want to tag along. He should be at the park by now. I said I'd meet him after school near the old bridge."

Tiffany's heart skipped a beat at the thought of seeing Zack. He was three years older than the girls and already a sophomore at State College.

*He has the dreamiest blue eyes.*

She remembered the first time she saw him.

\*    \*    \*

It was in fifth grade. Dorky Jimmy Fanöus left the class baseball bat at the far diamond behind the school. When it was discovered missing, Mr. Pierce asked the class, "Who's finished the test?" Tiffany, as usual, raised her hand.

"Then, Ms. Lincoln, please retrieve the bat that was left at the baseball diamond."

*Why do I have to walk all the way out there? I didn't leave it. It's not fair! I don't even like baseball. Just because I finished my test early and the rest are still working...*

Since she had no idea where it was, it took several minutes searching in the hot sun before she found the missing bat leaning against the fence by the home team bench. Hot, sweaty, and still angry, she trudged back toward the classroom, dragging the bat behind her.

As she approached the building, this tall, older, blond boy exited the rear stairs and crossed the quad. As they passed, he looked at her and smiled.

*Wow, is he cute!*

She stopped, mesmerized. He, of course, walked on unaffected. She watched until he disappeared into a side door.

It wasn't till later that she learned the cute guy was Zoe's older brother. So when Zoe asked her for help with math homework, she jumped at the chance. Zoe became Tiffany's best friend. Occasionally, when she visited Zoe's house, she'd see him and get the same thrill each time.

Of course, to Zack she was just his kid sister's friend.

\*    \*    \*

As they approached the bridge, they saw Zack stretched out on a nearby park bench. He was sound asleep, an open book resting on his chest. Zoe caught Tiffany's shoulder with her hand to stop her.

"This is too good," Zoe whispered. "Zack's always playing tricks on me. Now it's my turn to get back at him." She took off her backpack and placed it on the path. "Mom asked me to pick up a couple things from the store. This should work just fine," she said, removing a four-pack of toilet paper, breaking the plastic wrap, and pulling out a roll.

"What are you thinking?" Tiffany whispered back.

"Oh, nothing serious," she said. "I just thought we might wrap him up like he's in a cocoon. Then watch the fun."

"I don't think..." Tiffany began.

But Zoe cut her off. "It'll be a blast. Come on, I can't do it alone. I need your help. Pl... ease."

"But what if he gets mad?"

"Oh, he won't. And if he does, you can just say I made you do it."

Reluctantly, Tiffany agreed to help her friend. They quietly approached the bench with its sleeping occupant.

"You get on the other side," Zoe whispered. "I'll toss the roll over the bench to you. Then you roll it underneath back to me."

Toss over, roll under, over, under, all the while being careful not to make noise or touch Zack. Finally, the entire bench was wrapped in an overlapping layer of quilted white opaque paper.

Zoe motioned toward her backpack. "This deserves a treat. It wasn't on Mom's list, but I got some candy anyway." She pulled a Snickers bar from the pack, broke it in half, and handed part to Tiffany.

They settled against a nearby tree to watch the action. But there was no movement from under the shroud.

"This isn't any good," Zoe said. "He could sleep all afternoon. I better try something else."

She removed a large textbook from her pack, walked to the bench, and slammed the book hard on the bench backrest.

"What the..." came a voice from under the wrapping, followed by an arm pushing through to the surface. "Shit! What is this?"

The girls erupted in laughter at the sight and sound of Zack ripping his way to freedom. Scraps of TP clung to his clothes and arms, while streamers drifted into a growing pile around the bench.

Zoe laughed so hard she bent over double and finally sat down on her backpack to keep from falling over.

Still by the tree, Tiffany, laughing, took a bite of the Snickers and accidentally inhaled. The piece of candy lodged in her windpipe. She tried to cough, or cry out, but no sound came. She grabbed for her throat and reached toward her friend, but Zoe was too far away and busy watching her brother fight his way through the white paper snowstorm now engulfing the bench.

Tiffany staggered forward. Her vision was starting to blur and darken at the edges. A sound like rushing wind filled her ears. She dropped to her knees, still reaching for her friend as the world retreated down a long black tunnel.

Then, out of the darkness, she felt strong arms wrapped around her from behind, lifting her, supporting her. Fists pulled hard against her belly, once, twice. On the third pull, the candy dislodged. Welcome air rushed into her lungs.

She didn't remember being carried to the toilet paper-strewn bench, but when she opened her eyes, Zack's blue ones looked down at her. Zoe peered nervously over his shoulder.

"Breathing better now?" he asked. "Thought I might have to do mouth-to-mouth there for a moment." Then he laughed. "But you came around all by yourself."

*Passing out in front of Zack. How humiliating.*

"Hope that didn't hurt too much," Zack continued. "I had to Heimlich you pretty hard. You might be sore tomorrow."

*I've got to get out of here. This isn't the way I wanted Zack to see me.*

She tried to rise, but dizziness and Zack's hand on her shoulder stopped her.

"Whoa," he said. "Better rest a little longer. Don't want you blacking out again. I'm only good for one rescue a day. No repeats, please."

She lay back on the bench, began to shiver, and broke into a cold sweat. She could feel the moisture running down her neck and spine. Her bangs were plastered against her forehead.

*I probably have wet toilet paper stuck to me, too.*

"Zoe, put your pack under Tiffany's feet to raise them." Zack removed his windbreaker, placed it over her. "We wouldn't want your little friend going into shock."

*Little friend! Zack, I'm not a child anymore.* She wanted to say that, but could only nod weakly, lay her head back, and close her eyes.

Finally after a few minutes, the dizziness lifted and she began to feel more normal. Then she realized a crowd of spectators had formed around the bench.

*Oh, great! How embarrassing! All I need is for this to get back to school and I'll never live it down.*

"I think I can get up now," she said.

"You're sure?" Zack asked.

Holding Tiffany's hand, Zoe followed with, "We were really worried about you."

With Zack on one side and Zoe on the other, they steered Tiffany to Zack's car for the ride home.

* * *

"Time to wake up, dear." Tiffany's mother's call disturbed her dream.

Tiffany groaned. "Do I have to, Mom?"

"Yes you do. It's almost seven o'clock. I let you sleep in because of your accident yesterday, but school starts in an hour, and you don't want to be late."

*Wish I could just roll over and go back to sleep.*

In her dream, Zack had asked her to the prom and they kissed. The real Zack had taken her home and explained to her mother what had happened. Mom, of course, panicked, sent Zack and Zoe home, and immediately called Doctor Clark. Mom and Tiffany spent the rest of the afternoon at the clinic, until the doctor assured them everything was all right.

"Can't I just stay home today, pl... ease?"

"The doctor says you're fine. And you wouldn't want to lose your perfect attendance record, now would you? Shower and dress, I'll have breakfast on the table in twenty minutes."

*I'll bet the news will be all over school.*

* * *

Tiffany was right. The school buzzed with the incident. She tried to avoid crowds by moving quickly between classes, but everywhere she went, her friends pressured her to tell the 'whole story'. By lunchtime she just wanted to find an empty table away from the stares and sudden popularity.

"Hey Tiff, over here," Zoe called excitedly. "I saved you a place."

Tiffany groaned, then reluctantly carried her tray to the open spot at the busy table. *She is my best friend, after all.*

"It was so... cool, the way Zack saved you yesterday," she gushed as Tiffany sat down. "I've told everybody. My brother, the hero!"

Tiffany hunched over her lunch and tried to concentrate on her tuna salad sandwich as Zoe gave a blow-by-blow description of the incident to all their friends.

Finally, Zoe leaned close and whispered. "And Zack's being weird. First, he's been nice to me since yesterday, and then, this morning, he volunteered to give us a lift home. I didn't have to beg, or anything." She giggled. "I think he wants to see you again."

"Really? He said that?" Tiffany's heart skipped a beat. *Maybe fifteen minutes of fame isn't so bad after all.*

\*     \*     \*

The last period math class seemed to crawl on forever. Finally the bell rang. Tiffany loaded her books in her backpack and met her friend at the door for the short walk to the park.

Zack was waiting on the same bench, but this time he was awake. All evidence of yesterday's incident had been removed from the area. He rose as they approached.

"Hi, Tiffany," he said. "Are you feeling all right?" His heart-stopping blue eyes showed concern.

*Okay, Tiff, breathe. Act like it's no big deal, just normal conversation.*

"Sure, the doctor said there's no permanent damage."

"Good to hear. So, where would you two like to go?"

"We'll go to our house so Tiff and I can do homework," Zoe said. "But first, can we stop at McDonalds? I told some of some friends all about yesterday and they're dying to meet you."

Zack sighed. "I guess it's okay. Just for a few minutes though."

At McDonalds, Tiffany huddled in the far corner of the booth nursing a diet soda while a crowd of girls surrounded Zack. Zoe again repeated the rescue in full detail.

*Each time she tells the story, it's more exaggerated.* Tiffany looked at Zack. *He sure seems uncomfortable. I wonder if he's as tired of fame as I am. After this, he'll never going to want to see me again.*

\*     \*     \*

Tiffany was wrong. During the following week, Zack met the girls at the park every day to drive them home. Zack told her, now that he'd saved her life, he had a responsibility to protect her.

*Perfect. Now he's acting like my big brother.*

On the drive home, Zack and Zoe sat up front and did most of the talking while Tiffany moped in the back seat, feeling invisible. Zack dropped Tiffany at her house, then he and Zoe continued on home.

\*     \*     \*

"He likes you," Zoe said at lunch one day. "I can tell."

"He has a strange way of showing it. The only time I see him is in the rear view mirror of the car."

"He's really kinda shy around girls. There's a homecoming dance next month at the college, and he hasn't asked anybody yet. I've been dropping hints about you for days, but he's just not getting it. We may have to trick him into asking."

"I don't know," Tiffany replied. "The last trick we played on him didn't go so well."

"Sure it did. It got us rides home from school, didn't it?"

"Okay, what's your plan, Zoe?"

"Well... Tomorrow night, I'll tell him we have homework to do together at my house. Mom can fix us dinner. Then, later, he'll have to take you home. I'll stay behind. After that, it's up to you."

"That's a plan? Doesn't sound too great to me."

"Sure, you just get him talking at dinner about school and stuff. I'll mention the dance. That should do it."

\*     \*     \*

As planned, Tiffany ate with Zoe's family. During the meal, Tiffany asked Zack what college was like, and about the differences between college and high school. As they talked, Zoe dropped her hint about the dance. Zack immediately shifted the conversation to the football team's chances this season.

All the way home in the car, Zack was strangely quiet.

*Well, at least I get to sit in the front seat next to him, but our plan sucked.*

When they pulled up in front of her house, Zack shut off the engine and turned toward her.

"Don't think I don't know what you and my sister cooked up. It was pretty obvious during dinner."

*Oh no... here comes the rejection.*

"Actually..." Zack smiled. "I've been trying to come up with a way to ask you out. So... would you go to the college homecoming dance with me?"

*Would I! You bet. Cool it, Tiff.*

"I'd love to go, Zack."

"You know the first time I noticed you?" Zack confided. "It was about four years ago, at Parkside Grammar School. I was taking a note from the office to Mrs. Murphy in the library and I saw you walking across the schoolyard. At first, I wondered what you were doing out of class. Then I noticed you dragging that baseball bat like it was a boat anchor. You looked miserable. Then you saw me and got this deer-in-the-headlights expression. I had to smile. Still, there was something about you I just couldn't get out of my mind. Guess I just needed to wait a few years for you to grow up."

# George

"How are we feeling today, George?" Nurse Steve asked as he leaned over the bed at the Lakeside Extended Care Center.

*I don't know about 'we', but I'm feeling rotten*, George thought. Since the stroke had paralyzed his right side and taken his speech, he could only acknowledge by raising his left hand. He could also grunt, but that was all.

"Time for your bath and to get dressed for breakfast. It's Sunday. Your wife, Nancy, will probably be here later."

*Nancy,* George's inner voice said. If his paralyzed face could react he would have smiled.

George remembered the first time he'd seen Nancy.

\*     \*     \*

He'd just graduated from high school. Phil, his surfing buddy and fellow graduate, had suggested they rent a beach house for the summer. In the end, it took five surfing friends pooling their money to rent the tiny place on 37th Street, Newport Peninsula, close enough to walk to the pier. A perfect location for the local surf spots, and this gang of five was into surfing, big time.

That particular August morning, a south swell was running about five feet, but most of the regular surfboard breaks, 38th Street, 22nd Street, and the pier were pretty blown out by the onshore wind.

"Why don't we try body surfing at the Wedge?" Phil suggested. "It should be protected from the south wind by the jetty."

"Great idea," Jon, Phil's younger brother, agreed.

"Okay by me," George said. "It's too far to walk. Let me change and find keys. We can take my car."

George slipped out of his surfing baggies and into bun-huggers. The oversize surf trunks worked great on a surfboard to keep from getting wax rash, but racing Speedos were better adapted to bodysurfing. They didn't come off as easily. Grabbing a spare pair of Voit 'V-Duck' fins, he followed the others out to his fifty-four Ford woody.

At the Wedge, the wave at the takeoff peak looked to be about six-to-eight feet high with about ten bodysurfers in the water. Another fifty bystanders watched the action from the beach and jetty. The guys put on fins and duck walked or backed into the sea.

On George's second wave, he cut left, arm extended, hand planing on the steep wall of water. Suddenly, someone landed on his back. Arms and legs tangled. George tucked into a ball to protect himself as the wave tossed the pair over-the-falls and rolled them up the steep beach in a flow of whitewater. George spit out a mouthful of saltwater and sand, and blinked to clear the spray from his eyes. It was then he spotted something in the returning backwash and grabbed. It was a bathing suit top.

Several feet away, on her knees in the receding tide was a petite brunette, her arms instinctively placed across her chest. Sand clung to her skin and hair, her eyes wide in surprise.

"Did you lose something?" George asked, the top held behind his back.

"Yes," she replied, a look of panic on her very cute face.

"Could you use this?" he said, holding the article toward her. The relief in her expression was priceless.

"Please," she responded and extended one hand while still managing to cover her breasts.

He handed her the top. She turned to face the ocean to re-fasten it, only to discover the catch had been torn off. "Oh damn," she murmured. "It won't hook."

"Let me help," he volunteered.

"No, I think you've done enough already."

"Come on," he said, ignoring her jibe. "Sit down and hold your top in place while I remove your fins. I think we can find something to fix that suit. My car's right up there," he said, pointing to the woody.

"Bet you say that to all the topless girls you meet."

"No, you're the first. But if it works, I'll keep it. Makes a pretty good pickup line don't you think?" he laughed.

And she laughed with him.

"My name's George."

"I'm Nancy. Ordinarily I'd shake your hand, but under the circumstances..." She let the rest remain unsaid.

By the time they reached the car, George told himself he was in love. He found a shoelace to tie up the top. The repair wouldn't do to go in the water but would last till she got home.

*     *     *

"Okay, George." Nurse Steve's voice interrupted his thoughts. "Let's get you into your wheelchair and down to the dining room."

George had been in his 'dream world', as he called it, while his nurse had bathed, shaved, dressed him in sweat-pants, shirt, and diaper. Of course, he called the darn thing George's 'undergarments'. But George still thought of the underwear as a diaper or, at best, 'training pants'.

His dream was far better than real life in the nursing home. In his dreams, he could run and walk and talk and surf... and make love. In the real world, his active brain was trapped in a body that did not respond and thoughts that could not be made into words. He hated it.

Steve wheeled him to the dining room. On the table was a plate with three globs on it. One was brown, one yellow, and the last white. The doctors feared he would choke on solid food, so all his meals were puréed into unrecognizable pabulum. The nurse placed a spoon in his hand.

*My test for the day.*

Nurse Steve watched as, with trembling movements of his left hand, George scooped some yellow stuff from the plate and slowly, ever so slowly, raised it to his mouth.

*Okay, it's eggs, I think.*

Every day, George proved he could feed himself. It was his bid for independence. Steve was nice and let him continue for some time on his own. Most of the other staff only let him finish a bite or two before taking the spoon.

Following breakfast, patients sat in the hall outside their rooms while the cleaning was done. George's mind drifted back to Nancy and their first real date. Disneyland, it had been Disneyland... and the Matterhorn.

\* \* \*

They'd been seeing each other for about a month, mostly meeting at the beach. He tried to teach her to ride a board, but she still preferred body surfing. He had taken a photo of her angling across a wave. On it she had written in permanent marker: "Nancy Stratton hanging two at The Wedge." It was their little joke. He framed it and placed it over his bed.

Summer was ending. He would be going to college and she back to high school. He wanted to ask her out on a real date. It would have to be somewhere really special. Then one day, the idea came to him.

*Disneyland! Now that's somewhere special. I can do it. I've several half-full magic kingdom books from previous visits, and Phil's father works maintenance there. He could sign us in. I'll owe Phil big time, but it'll be worth it.*

Happily, she agreed to go.

The day at Disneyland turned out to be even better than he'd hoped. They walked the park, and George splurged for dinner at Blue Bayou, watching the passing pirate boats and fireflies. They finished the evening watching the fireworks from Carnation Plaza. But the best was the Matterhorn.

He'd been on the ride many times, but this was her first. He guided her to the bobsled and got in, moving to the rear of the seat. She climbed in and slid back against him while the attendant fastened the belts over them. She settled against his chest and laid her head against his shoulder. The scent of her perfume flooded his nose. He breathed deeply.

They had bodysurfed waves together, she in a skimpy bikini and he in racing Speedos, but now, fully dressed, so close together in the bobsled...

*Damn,* he thought, *I'm getting an erection. Maybe if I tuck my hips back, she won't notice.*

The sled started forward and rolled down to the lift. The drive chain caught the car and jerked it forward pressing her even harder into him.

*She must have felt that!*

Just before the top of the lift, he got his answer; she reached up, turned his head toward her and kissed him, hard, on the lips. They clung together all the way down. He kept his hands tightly around her waist and fought the urge to reach down to her hips or up to cup her breasts.

From there he took Nancy immediately to the Fantasyland Skyway where a couple could have four minutes of uninterrupted kisses before the gondola arrived at Tomorrowland station.

\*    \*    \*

A hand on George's shoulder interrupted his reminiscence.

"Hi, honey," Nancy said. "How do you feel today?"

He gave her a left-handed thumbs-up sign. During the months of convalescence, they had developed their own code of hand signals.

"Would you like to take a walk around the lake? It's a beautiful day," she suggested. He nodded.

"The sun's really bright today. I'd better get your fisherman's hat. Wouldn't want you to get sunburned," she said as she headed toward his room to retrieve the floppy canvas hat he wore when outdoors. One loss during his long convalescence was his tan. Now his pale skin needed to be protected whenever he went outside.

Nancy pushed the wheelchair the two blocks to Lakeview Park, his favorite place. Here, they watched the ducks and other waterfowl. Often she sat on a bench, his chair beside it. They held hands, and she told him of all the church and neighborhood activities, the latest on their daughter, her husband, and the grandkids, the friends who'd called or stopped by, anything she thought he might like to hear. He signaled his interest in topics and responded to each with a hand gesture or a grunt. Finally, they needed to return to the home.

Nancy fed him lunch. She was so much more patient than the staff. They were often hurried and stuffed food into his mouth too fast. She talked to him and let him chew and swallow each bite before offering another. Following the meal, she kissed him goodbye, and he watched her exit through the front doors to the parking lot. Steve pushed him back to his room for his afternoon nap.

*   *   *

Right after George's college graduation, they were married. He was twenty-two, she twenty. His folks gave them a trip to Hawaii as a honeymoon present, and it was wonderful. They hiked into a distant waterfall off the Hana Road and found a secluded pool. Swimming to the far side, George climbed the low cliff and made a daring leap from twenty feet into the inviting water below. As he surfaced, blinking to clear his eyes, déjà vu, a swimsuit top floated by, but this time it was followed by a bikini bottom. It didn't take long for him to get the message, shed his own trunks, and join his wife.

They returned to Hawaii many times during the following years to enjoy the ocean and beautiful surroundings. First they visited as a couple, then as a family, after first-born Karen arrived, followed two years later by Max. They all loved the sea and spent as much time in the water as possible.

The years of images replayed while he slept.

\*　　\*　　\*

"Dinnertime, George," Nurse Steve said as he entered the room. "Time to get you up." He lifted George off the bed into the chair for the ride to the dining hall.

George sat with his meal before him. Steve was helping another patient and would be a while. George stuck his finger in the chocolate pudding and with slow and shaky movements, spelled the word 'pen' on the tabletop.

When Steve saw it he said, "You want a pen and paper?"

A thumbs-up.

"Okay, but first you have to eat some dinner."

Steve generally went off duty after dinner. But this night he stayed, holding the steno pad steady while George painstakingly formed each letter. It took a long time.

> Dearest Nancy
>
> I loved you every moment.
> Doctors think I don't hear.
> Say kidneys fail. Not much time.
> Left instructions Grandma's Bible
> Phil 1:3-4
> I love you

George didn't wake the next morning.

\*　　\*　　\*

It took Nancy several days to locate his grandmother's Bible in the study. In it she found a folded sheet of paper. It read:

## GEORGE'S POEM

Bury me not near the old oak tree,
In a prison tomb, dirt over me.
But leave my spirit to swim free,
And cast my ashes out to sea.
To rise like mist in the morning sun
And ride the swells till the day is done.

She also read the verse:

*I thank God every time I remember you.*
*And every time I pray for you all. I always*
*pray with joy.* Philippians 1: 3-4

# Sheila

Sheila closed her eyes and leaned back on the park bench. Extending her arms and clasping her hands behind her neck, she raised her face to the sky to feel the sun's warmth on her cheeks. She inhaled deeply and slowly let the air escape through her teeth. For an instant, seated here on the bench, she could block out the rest of her world. At least for a little while.

The call from her father the previous night had shocked her. It had been four years since she'd spoken to her parents. Not since that last time. The meeting still haunted her memory.

\* \* \*

"Get out of this house. Get out of my sight. I never want to see you ever again!" her mother had screamed. "No daughter of mine would ever act this way. It's against all God's teachings."

"You're not being fair. Bekka and I love each other and want to be together," Sheila had pleaded, but her mother would hear no more and stormed out leaving Rebecca, Sheila, and her dad at the kitchen table. Her father, as usual, said nothing. He just stared at his coffee cup and looked sad.

"Maybe we should go," Rebecca suggested after a long pause.

Her father looked up. "Sheila dear, your mother will come around... eventually. Just be patient."

It was Sheila's turn to be angry. "This is who I am, Dad. Does Mom think I have a choice to change? Come on, Bekka, we're leaving."

\*　　\*　　\*

She had first met Rebecca Norwood when they worked together at the Chrysler dealership. Bekka worked in the finance department when Sheila was hired as the new receptionist. Their friendship had grown during daily noon walks and lunches in the park. They began visiting the local Ralphs for prepared food and ate at a picnic table overlooking the lake. Both enjoyed the outdoors and found they had much in common.

At the time, Rebecca was in an abusive marriage. Her husband was an alcoholic, although he didn't think he had a problem. When drunk, he had attacked and beaten her several times. After the third beating, Rebecca feared for her life and resolved to file for divorce. Sheila helped her plan her escape.

One Friday, while Paul was at work, they packed Bekka's belongings. Sheila let her stay at her apartment temporarily, just until she could find a place of her own. Paul showed up at the dealership on Monday. But by then, a restraining order had been served. With several large salesmen present, he was quickly persuaded to leave. A month later, Rebecca discovered she was pregnant. A final parting gift from her no-good husband.

They attended childbirth classes together. Rebecca introduced Sheila as her partner and no one there seemed to think it unusual.

Megan Virginia Norwood was born six-pounds, two-ounces, twenty-one inches long, at Memorial Hospital. By then, the women's relationship had changed into much more than a mere friendship. After Megan's birth, Sheila continued to work at the dealership while Bekka stayed home with the baby. Without Rebecca's income, finances were tight.

In desperation, Sheila turned to her parents for help. Her conservative and stern Christian mother disapproved of her daughter's lifestyle and refused. Her father had reluctantly sided with his wife.

Sheila took a second job waitressing at a restaurant on weekends, and the two women and the child squeaked by. But she hadn't spoken to her mother since.

\*     \*     \*

Her father's phone call last night brought back all the bitter memories.

"Sheila dear," he'd said, "your mother's very ill. The cancer has spread to her liver. The doctors say she hasn't much time left."

"Did she ask for me?" Sheila inquired. *Please say, "Yes."*

"No. She won't admit it, but I know she wants to see you. Please come, even if only for my sake."

"I'll think about it, Daddy."

"I love you, little girl."

"You too, Daddy. Goodbye."

*   *   *

Her thoughts were interrupted by Bekka's arrival carrying a lunch basket, with four-year-old Megan tagging along behind. Together the women set their meal out on the picnic table.

"Can I feed the ducks? Can I please?" Megan pleaded. "I want to feed the ducks."

"She's been pestering me all day," Bekka complained, extracting a textbook from her oversize purse. "I haven't been able to get any studying done, and I have a final at school tonight."

"Okay Meg, you come with Mimi, and we'll let Mama read."

Bekka smiled appreciatively before turning to her open book.

"Oh goody, Mimi. Can we feed the ducks like always?" Megan smiled up at her second mother, the one she called Mimi.

"I'm sorry, Meg, but we can't today."

"Why?"

"Because it will make them sick."

"Why?"

"See the sign over there? It says, 'Do not feed the ducks.' There's a bad disease in the lake water. And when people feed bread to the ducks, they get sick and die. We wouldn't want that to happen, would we?"

"No," Megan said tentatively, her lower lip thrust out in a pout.

"Well then, bring your bologna sandwich. Sit over here by me and I'll pour your milk."

Megan finished half her sandwich, and then jumped down from the bench.

"Can I see the ducks now?" she asked.

"Yes, you may. Just don't go near the water. You know the rules."

"Okay, Mimi," she said and started toward the shoreline.

"That little scamp." Bekka smiled, looking up from her book. "She took the other half of her sandwich with her. She's going to toss it in the lake."

The scream brought Sheila to her feet and quickly down the hill to meet a hysterical Megan running toward her, the half sandwich clutched in her fist. Sheila grabbed the child. Tiny arms wrapped around her neck and a head buried itself into her shoulder.

"Meg, what's the matter?" she asked the distraught youngster.

"I didn't do it, Mimi. I didn't feed the duck," the little girl said between sobs.

Sheila looked toward the edge of the lake and saw the remains of a mallard floating head-down near the shore. It appeared to Sheila to have been dead for some time.

"It's okay, Megan. We know it's not your fault," she soothed, holding the child softly against her until the sobbing subsided.

"Will they all die?" Meg asked with a sniff.

"No honey, not all of them. The park people put up the signs to save the birds. Look out there." Sheila pointed to several ducks swimming farther out. "See, they're okay."

Sheila held and softly reassured Megan for several minutes till the tears stopped. They returned to their lunch. Back at the table, as she told a concerned Bekka what had happened, an incident from her own past came to mind.

\* \* \*

She remembered when she was about Megan's age, thunderstorms scared her. One night when Daddy was away, a big one came up. Her room went bright with each flash followed by the crash of thunder. Sheila hid under the covers as long as she could. Then she crept in tears to her parents' room. Mother had always insisted Sheila sleep in her own bed.

"I'm not having any child sleep with us," she'd often told her husband as Sheila listened. That night though, her mother held her through the storm till she fell asleep. Mother even got her to count, "One-thousand-one, one-thousand-two..." between the bright flash and the thunder crack to tell how far away the lightning was.

"Now, don't tell your father where you slept," her mother said the next morning. "It will be our secret."

\* \* \*

"I need to see my mother tonight," Sheila said to Bekka as they packed the lunch basket. "You have class, so Megan will have to come with me. My father can watch her while I visit Mom." Bekka raised an eyebrow but didn't say a word.

\* \* \*

As Sheila entered her mother's room, she hardly recognized the woman sitting in a wheelchair next to the bed. The once-auburn hair was now gray and unkempt. Instead of a neat dress, she wore a flannel nightgown and tan cotton housecoat. She looked old, tiny, and frail.

"Hello, Mother," Sheila said softly.

"Came here to see if I was dead yet?" The voice was softer, but none of the venom was gone.

"No, Mother, I came to see you alive." *This is a mistake, I shouldn't have come.*

"Well, I'm here, but not for long. So the doctors say. Still with that... woman? What's her name?"

"Rebecca, Mother. It's Rebecca, and yes we're still together."

They remained in silence for a moment, as if neither knew what to say.

A small head poked around the corner. And a little body ran over to peek out from behind Sheila's knees.

"Who's this?" her mother demanded.

"She's Rebecca's daughter."

"Step out here, child. I want to see you."

Megan looked up. Sheila nodded, moved aside, and gently prodded the child forward.

"Come here. I won't bite. What is your name? Speak up now."

Megan took a deep breath, raised to her full height and said, "It's Megan Virginia Norwood, and I'm four years old."

Mother's gaze shifted from the child to Sheila, who gave a small nod.

"I'm pleased to meet you Megan Virginia Norwood. Did you know my name is also Virginia? Now, you come here and give your grandmother a hug." She looked to Sheila. "You too. We've lost a great deal of time already."

Embracing both her mother and Megan, Sheila looked up to see her father in the doorway, tears streaming down his face to match her own.

*How strange and wonderful*, Sheila thought, *that a little child, not even biologically related, could have brought my family back together.*

# Carlos

Carlos pulled the Hustler Super Z to a stop in the shade of the eucalyptus and pressed the motor kill switch. The roar of the riding mower engine ceased. He removed his noise-canceling  earmuffs and wiped the sweat from his face and neck with his hand towel.

*It's got to be close to lunchtime,* he thought. *Must be ninety-five degrees out here, and I still have the whole west side to cut.*

Carlos pushed the twin control sticks aside, stepped from the machine and walked the few feet to the parked maintenance truck. He glanced across the upper lake as he pulled a paper cup from the dispenser and poured cool water from the spout on the cooler tied onto the tailgate. He downed the first cupful in a couple of big swigs, and then filled a second to sip more slowly. Reaching behind the seat in the cab, he extracted two aspirin tablets from the half-empty bottle.

*Seems like I always have a headache on grass cutting day. But today the pain is even worse. Hell, you're seventy years old. What ya expect?*

He sat on the edge of the tailgate, swallowed the tablets, finished the cup, and looked out over the park.

Several fishermen lined the far bank like birds on a wire, each staking out his own bit of territory.

*They won't catch much today. The Fish and Game folks aren't scheduled to deliver the next shipment of trout and catfish till next Thursday. Lake's pretty well fished out till then. The only ones who seem to know the fish-stocking schedule are the cormorants. They always manage to show up en masse the week following a delivery.*

In the distance, he could hear the other lawnmower, twin to the one Carlos used, working the south lawn. Together, he and Tom would cover the entire park before dark. This was the last time Carlos would cut grass on the Hustler. As of Friday, he'd be retired. Next week, Tom and someone else would share the job.

*Mandatory retirement. That's what they call it. Still feels like I'm being pushed out.*

Carlos rubbed his forehead, blinked to clear his vision, and looked at his watch.

*Yep, eleven-thirty. Time to eat.*

He pulled the metal lunchbox from behind the driver's seat. Settling against the tire on the shady side of the pickup, he opened the container and lifted the napkin to see what Maria had packed.

Carlos identified each item: two bologna sandwiches, an apple, bag of Fritos, and two homemade chocolate-chip cookies. The thermos held milk.

While he ate, he noted the model sailboat club unloading their radio-controlled craft on the peninsula jutting into the lower lake. They'd be racing again today. Along with the regular old-timers was the young kid, the troublemaker. He'd heard the boy was almost expelled from school. Then the old guy in the white pants and Panama hat interested him in RC sailing.

*Seems like those two are buddies.*

Farther up the path, the noontime walkers were starting their laps. Several young mothers with children in tow arrived at the playground.

*Just a normal day,* he thought. *Will I miss it next week when I'm no longer a part of this? I've been here for almost forty-five years. It'll be different.*

Carlos finished his second sandwich, and picked up the apple just as Tom pulled up on his mower and cut the engine.

"Nice o' you to wait-up," Tom said, as he joined him in the shade of the vehicle.

"You know, next week you'll have to meet the Muellers at four o'clock every day. Marian's counting on you to keep up with James on his laps," Carlos reminded Tom for the umpteenth time.

"Sure, sure I'll remember. You'll come back to visit, won't you? I mean, the place just isn't going to be the same without you."

"Well, my Maria's been talking about moving back east to be near the grandkids. I don't really want to leave the area, but she can be pretty persuasive."

"Yeah, you mean like the timeshare she insisted on buying in Virginia Beach so she could be near the kids? Then they moved to Chicago. How many times did you use it?"

"I think we did once, about ten years ago. Not such a bargain, was it?" Carlos chuckled, then wiped his hands. "Well, better get back to work. Lots of grass left to cut."

He stowed the empty lunchbox behind the pickup seat and turned toward his machine.

*        *        *

Late in the afternoon, they drove the mowers up the ramp onto the waiting trailer. Tom would return the trailer to the maintenance yard at the end of the day. Carlos filled another paper cup with water from the tailgate cooler and swallowed two more aspirin. It was then he noticed a man walking slowly up the path near the lower lake, some fifty yards away.

The man stood tall and straight, but his steps were slow and deliberate. He stopped often and kept to the side of the path avoiding the other folks in the park. His shoulder-length hair was matted and gray, as was his beard. His threadbare clothes, the color of soot, looked to have been worn, unwashed, for many days.

*The gray man. I think I've seen him before. I just don't remember when. Amazing, he's standing in the middle of a green park on a bright cloudless afternoon, and yet appears untouched by the sun.*

Carlos watched him carefully avoid a group of young mothers and children sitting on and around a park bench. He finally settled cross-legged with his back against the trunk of an ancient eucalyptus overlooking the water. Nearby, several children, between two and seven years, walked the lake edge causing the resting ducks and geese to seek the safety of the water. One young boy carried a stick to assist the water fowl on their journey.

Carlos sighed, "I better go down there and tell them not to harass the birds."

Before Carlos could move, the boy reached too far with the stick, slipped, and fell into the water. Carlos ran toward the splash, as did one of the mothers. She followed the boy into waist-deep water and grabbed him, but the muddy bottom was slippery. Her shoes slid and she couldn't reach the bank. Suddenly, the gray man was there at the edge, and grasped the woman's extended forearm. He held it until Carlos arrived to pull both mother and child to safety. The woman had lost a shoe and was wet and muddy from the waist down. The boy was soaked through and coughed up some water before starting to cry. A crowd gathered around them.

"If you ever do that again..." the mother exclaimed. Her voice was harsh, but the way she hugged the boy so tightly disproved her words.

After a time, the crying subsided.

"Thank you, oh thank you," the woman repeated to Carlos.

Tom arrived with an emergency thermal blanket from the first aid kit in the pickup and placed it around the rescued pair. They moved to a nearby bench.

Carlos looked around, but the gray man had disappeared. He then realized he was out of breath, and his heart was pounding.

*You're getting too old to run like that.*

He rested at the far end of the bench while Tom wrote down information on the mishap for the logbook. Parks and Recreation Department would want a full report of the incident.

Tom suggested they call an ambulance to have the boy checked out, but the mother declined. "I'll take him home. We'll see our own doctor tomorrow," she assured them.

Tom walked the woman and child to her car and watched them drive away. The crowd slowly dispersed until only Tom and Carlos were left. They climbed the hill to the pickup and finished loading.

"Strange," Carlos said. "Another man held them until I arrived, but I couldn't find him afterward. Did you see where he went?"

"What? I didn't see anyone. You were the only one anywhere near them."

"But, before I caught her hand, didn't you see a man in gray holding her arm?"

"Nope, nobody there but you," Tom insisted. "I'll take the truck with the mowers. You bring the pickup. I'll see you back at the maintenance yard."

Carlos watched as Tom drove off. He pinched his forehead between thumb and fingers and shut his eyes tight, before taking a deep breath and exhaling slowly between clenched teeth.

*I'm tired*, he thought, *and the headache is worse.*

Carlos opened the door, slid behind the steering wheel, and reached to turn the ignition. It was then he noticed the gray man seated again at the old eucalyptus.

"Hell," he murmured. "I better get to the bottom of this." He exited the truck and approached the figure.

"There's no overnight camping in the park. You'll have to leave when it gets dark."

"We'll be gone long before then."

Carlos looked for another person, but saw no one. *Better change the subject.*

"You know, you saved the woman and little boy today. They might have drowned if you hadn't grabbed her and kept her from sliding further into the lake."

"Sometimes I like doing that," the man answered, gazing out at the lake. His deep voice spoke barely above a whisper but radiated power. "Besides, it wasn't their time."

"But, no one saw you. Except me."

"Anyone can see me if they really try. Some see only a tramp or drifter to be pitied, scorned, or avoided. But most just don't pay any attention. It's as if I'm invisible. I like it that way."

The man looked up, and Carlos felt a chill as gray, deep-set, eyes focused on him. "Very few see who I really am. You saw me because you're always watchful for the safety of everyone in the park. It's why I chose this look. I knew you'd notice."

"You knew I'd notice? I don't understand."

"Well, what if I showed up in a black hooded robe and carried a scythe. Would it make a difference?"

"If it wasn't Halloween, I'd think you were crazy."

The man chuckled, "You'd be wrong."

"What did you mean 'not their time'?" Carlos asked.

"Everyone has a time. You know, like Ecclesiastes, 'to everything there is a season... A time to be born and a time to die...'"

"I know the verse."

"Well, you see me now because it's time. How do you feel?"

Carlos felt his forehead. *Back in the truck, I was exhausted and my head ached. Now I feel fine, rested even. What's going on?*

The man pushed against the tree trunk to get to his feet. "It's getting late," he said. "We should be going."

"But what... what about my Maria and the family? I can't leave now."

"They'll be all right. You've seen to her security. And Maria will not be alone for long. Your kids will take care of that."

Carlos looked back at the pickup parked on the hill. In the cab, he could see a man slumped in the driver's seat. His gaze panned slowly across the park. The sun, dipping toward the horizon, cast long shadows of the trees upon the lake. The water rippled on the slight breeze. Ducks and geese huddled in groups along the bank, awaiting nightfall. He'd spent so much of his life here.

"Do you think I could watch a last sunset?"

"Normally we'd leave immediately. But... Well, I guess so. I have it on good authority the sunset will be spectacular tonight."

# Acknowledgements

Without those listed below, this book would not have been possible. Thank you to:

**Tom Hill**—My good friend and walking partner. Thanks for introducing me to the park and encouraging me keep the chapters coming.

**Kuniko Igo**—*Arigato gozaimasu* for inviting us to your home in Mikamo, Japan and sharing your family with us as your *gaijin* friends.

The late **Wayne McKibbin**, whose vintage Stratocaster and songwriting ability came to mind while watching another guitarist practice in the park.—You're loved and missed.

**Dr. Christopher Coppola**—Thanks for all the military jargon and inspiration. Your own real life story, *Made a Difference for That One—A Surgeon's Letters Home from Iraq,* compiled by Meredith Coppola, tells of the true heroism and compassion of our soldiers serving in foreign lands far better than I.

**Capistrano Beach Care Center**—The gentle treatment and genuine caring of your staff made my mother-in-law's last years the best possible. You demonstrated what nursing homes should be like.

**Lagunita Writers' Group**—Your suggestions and patient encouragement helped make these stories come alive. And special thanks to **Martha Anderson** our hostess, leader, and the best cookie maker around.

Special thanks to **Lorna Collins**—You kept after me to finish the #@*~ book. Your persistence, editing excellence, and encouragement brought this project to fruition. I couldn't have done it without you. I love you so much.

# About the Book

*Lakeview Park* is a work of fiction, but the park is real.

Working in an engineering office on a computer left little opportunity for exercise. So, for ten years, my friend, Tom, and I walked around the actual lake in Tri-City Park in Orange County, California during our lunch hour.

Often, I would observe others sailing model boats, fishing, picnicking, running, jogging, or walking. Watching these people became the inspiration for the characters in the stories. With few exceptions, I never spoke to them or learned their real life histories. It was much more fun to create stories from my imagination.

Oh, but the ghost may, in fact, be real. Her story is loosely based on newspaper accounts and hearsay about the spirit of a woman said to haunt the park.

# About the Author

Larry K. Collins won his first literary awards as a student at Alhambra High School in Alhambra, California, when two of his short stories were published in the school's literary magazine, *The Silver Pen*. For the most part, his creative writing was put on hold during his career as an engineer. However, he wrote many proposals and the training manual for petrochemical engineering design for his company.

Between 1997 and 2001, Larry and his wife, Lorna, worked on the Universal Studios Japan theme park in Osaka. When they returned, they wrote their memoir of that experience, *31 Months in Japan: The Building of a Theme Park*, published in 2005. This book was a finalist for the 2006 EPPIE Award for nonfiction ebook of the year and was also chosen as one of Rebeccas Reads best nonfiction books of 2005.

Larry and Lorna collaborated again on two mysteries: *Murder... They Wrote*, published in 2009, and *Murder in Paradise*, published in 2011. The latter is a finalist for the 2012 EPIC eBook of the year for mystery. These books are set in Hawaii, requiring frequent trips for research.

After a successful engineering career, Larry is now retired and living in Dana Point, California, where he surfs nearly every day and writes often. He and Lorna are currently working on at least two more books in the mystery series.

With this collection, he has returned to his roots as a short story author.

In addition to their writing, Lorna and Larry are frequent conference speakers and are available to address book clubs and other groups. Contact them through their website: www.lornalarry.com.